Crickets chirped in a cheerful chorus in the grass and Rae listened to the sounds, feeling peace settle inside her. Then there was another sound, the sound of quiet steps in the grass.

'Are you avoiding me?' Jason's voice. She turned to face him, stiffening with resentment. She didn't want him here in the quiet of the night, disturbing her peace.

'You want the truth, or shall I be polite?'

His mouth quirked. 'By all means, the truth, please.'

'Well, yes, as a matter of fact, I am avoiding you.'

'Why?'

'You make me uncomfortable.'

JAVA NIGHTS

BY

KAREN VAN DER ZEE

MILLS & BOON LIMITED
ETON HOUSE   18–24 PARADISE ROAD
RICHMOND   SURREY   TW9 1SR

First published in Great Britain 1990
by Mills & Boon Limited

© Karen van der Zee 1990

Australian copyright 1990
Philippine copyright 1990
This edition 1990

ISBN 0 263 76661 6

Set in 10 on 11 pt Linotron Times
01-9004-53930
Typeset in Great Britain by Centracet, Cambridge
Made and printed in Great Britain

PROLOGUE

ALL Rae knew was his name: *Steel*. No first name, no Mr. She had never met him, nor seen him. She had never spoken to him, nor heard his voice. Yet in her mind she had a picture of him as vivid as reality. She knew what he looked like—dark, tall, with cold grey eyes and a hard, cruel mouth. He was power-hungry, unscrupulous, ruthless, mercenary, and he had ruined her life.

Matt was dead. Matt, her husband, her lover, her friend.

It was all Steel's fault. She could not escape the thought. She couldn't help but connect all the events, a chain of incidents leading back to Steel's forcing Matt out of the contract, out of Indonesia.

If he hadn't forced Matt out, they wouldn't have had to return to the States, hopes and dreams shattered. Matt would not have been so miserable those last few months. He would not have been drinking so much. He would not have drowned.

Rae looked at herself in the mirror. She hardly recognised the woman gazing back at her. Hazel eyes looked dull and lifeless and too large for her face. Her hair, normally a lively shock of short chestnut curls, drooped limply around her head. Her skin was sallow, her body painfully thin. She looked sick, but she didn't care any more. Nothing mattered. Her life lay in ruins and she wished she were dead.

If Steel had not been in search of more power and money and glory, she would not be a widow at twenty-five.

CHAPTER ONE

THE panic didn't hit until Rae boarded the tiny propeller-driven aircraft in Jakarta. The air was hot and humid, and thick with unfamiliar smells. Her heart was beating too fast and for a moment she had the urge to turn around and flee. But her feet kept moving forward, one step at a time up the hot metal stairs until she was inside.

All through the seemingly endless journey from New York to Indonesia, she had pushed back her fear and uncertainties. But now there was no turning back. This small, decrepit-looking plane would land her back in the small town of Semarang in less than an hour, back to a past that held both joy and pain.

It was probably the stupidest thing she had ever done, yet she had known from the beginning that she would come back to the Far East one day. Only she hadn't known she would come alone. She pushed back the sudden pain. Two years now. Two years since Matt had died.

Ten minutes into the flight, a dark-eyed hostess— small, thin, elegant and beautifully made-up—offered her a glass of hot tea and a small cardboard box. The woman made her feel like Cinderella before the fairy godmother had done her thing. Her clothes were rumpled, her make-up smudged, her skin sticky.

'*Terima kasih*,' Rae said, the words coming back with surprising ease. She took a careful sip from the hot brew, grimacing at the syrupy taste. She'd forgotten how sweet the Indonesians liked their tea, their snacks, their soft drinks. She opened the white box, finding a pink, glutinous piece of cake and a small bar of chocolate.

The time passed in a blur. She was too nervous to read—besides, she'd done nothing but read for the past two days. Her stomach felt as if she'd swallowed a ton of gravel. Next to her an Indonesian businessman in suit and tie was reading the English language *Jakarta Times*, silent and absorbed. She wondered why anybody in his right mind would wear a suit and tie in the tropics.

She looked out of the window, seeing the glittering Java Sea below and the glorious green of the rice paddies on the land, and finally the town of Semarang off on the right with its red-tiled roofs and crowded streets. It looked just like she remembered it, but of course two and a half years was not such a long time.

A wave of heat, damp and dense, washed over Rae as she walked out of the plane on to the shimmering tarmac. Moisture exploded out of her skin, and for a moment she could not breathe. She would have to get used to that again, the relentless tropical heat and the eternal stickiness of skin and clothes.

Nicky was waiting for her as she had promised, wearing a flamboyant red dress, her face bright with expectation. She still looked the same, with her bright green eyes, and long blonde hair tied on top of her head in an untidy, loose fashion with frizzy curls escaping everywhere. She hugged Rae hard.

'I'm so glad you're here!' she said, stepping back and examining Rae with a smile. 'I can't believe it, you really came! You look better than when I saw you in New York last year. You've gained some weight. Lord, I was worried about you! You looked like something from a refugee camp! How was your flight? Rotten, of course, it can't be anything else. You were nuts not to stay overnight in Hong Kong or Tokyo.'

Rae smiled. 'Shut up, Nicky,' she said mildly, knowing it wasn't something her friend did easily. Nicky had
an exuberant, extravagant nature that was quite
untameable.

Nicky grinned. 'Sorry. Just can't help myself. 'OK,
let's get out of here.'

Tuki, the driver, who'd hovered in the background
until Nicky introduced him, took Rae's two suitcases
and they found their way into the car park to the apple-
green Mitsubishi van.

All through the fifteen-minute ride to the house,
Nicky talked. Rae listened as she watched the chaotic
traffic—motorcycles with three or more people on
board, trucks overloaded with baskets, mattresses, or
produce in precarious balance, a bullock cart rumbling
along sedately in the middle of it all.

'You'll have all the privacy you want,' Nicky was
saying. 'You can eat with us any time you want, or you
can eat in your own room—whatever you like. We've
had a fan put in on the veranda and we got some rattan
furniture set up. The school paid for all of it, of course.
It's a nice place, and I'm sure you'll like it.'

'I know the place, Nicky,' Rae smiled. 'I used to
come to your house on a regular basis, remember? I
know your guest apartment is perfect. Relax, will you?'

'I just want you to be happy here.'

Rae squeezed Nicky's hand, saying nothing. Happy.
She wondered often if she would ever be happy again.
It was two years since Matt had died, and the worst
pain had dulled, yet true happiness had eluded her.
Time, she thought, I just need time.

'How's David?' she asked, and Nicky grimaced.

'Getting nuttier by the day. He says we need children
so he can become a respectable father, but you know
me. First I want to be famous.'

Rae laughed. 'Then you really won't have time.
You'll be in your dark-room day and night and your

skin will turn green and your hair will fall out and David will run away screaming when he sees you.'

'You're so encouraging,' Nicky said drily.

Several cars were parked in the driveway when they arrived at the house.

'The P.T. L'Or order came in,' Nicky said, grimacing. 'Steak and strawberries melting all over my dining-room floor.'

Once a month the foreign community in Semarang banded together and sent in a food order to a Jakarta-based food import company servicing hotels and restaurants: steak from the US or Australia; frozen peaches from the US; butter and cheese from New Zealand; cheese, pâtés, mustards and other delicacies from France. Packed in dry ice, the order was delivered to Nicky's house, from where people would pick up their various items, hopefully before the frozen ones had defrosted in the heat.

Several people were in the dining-room sorting out the order.

'Attention, attention!' Nicky said loudly. 'May I introduce to you my friend, Rae Smith, fresh off the plane, here to rescue our school's ESL programme!'

Rae had taught at the Semarang International School the year she and Matt had lived in the town. Now, with a fresh degree in English as a Second Language, she was back. The school was located in a house, painted and furnished by the parents. At the moment twenty-three students from eleven different countries were getting educated in the blue-painted rooms. The language was English, which was not the mother tongue of more than half the students. Helping these students cope with learning English as fast as possible so they could keep up with their studies was Rae's new job.

Several faces now turned to Rae curiously. Only one was familiar. With a squeal of delight, Josie hurled her voluminous frame forwards and hugged Rae. Josie had never lacked enthusiasm and warmth. 'I want you to come and see my baby as soon as you have time,' she said to Rae, who promised. Hands were extended, introductions made. There was a Swiss woman with short blonde hair and two rambunctious sons, a balding Bavarian with dark-rimmed glasses, and a tall American with penetrating blue eyes and a firm hand-shake. His name was Jason Grant. His smile was cool and polite, yet Rae felt a sudden hot surge of electric-ity, as if somehow something between them had con-nected, a secret awareness shivering unbidden under the surface. Good lord, what's the matter with me? she thought, wiping the damp hair out of her face. The room seemed extraordinarily warm, even with the fan swooping overhead at full speed. Fatigue could cause strange chemical reactions in the brain; hadn't she read that somewhere?

Rae wished she'd had a chance to shower and change before meeting these people. She felt unclean—she *was* unclean, no doubt smelling of aircraft, stale food and cigarette smoke. Her hair was a mess, and her clothes looked as if she'd slept in them, which she had, sort of.

Nicky moved towards the door. 'Jason, you're coming for dinner, right? Bring Anouk if you want to.'

'Thanks, maybe I will.'

Everyone went back to sorting out the food and Nicky took Rae down the hall to the guest apartment.

'Do whatever you want,' Nicky said, tucking a loose curl behind her ear. 'Sleep, or come up to the veranda for a cold drink. We won't eat until seven or so, but Ibu can bring you something here if you'd rather not join us.'

'Thanks.' Rae glanced around the room. The window air-conditioner was running and the place was cool and welcoming. There was a bedroom with an adjoining bathroom, and a sitting-room with a door leading on to a small, private veranda overlooking the side yard with its gnarled frangipani tree and the banana plants in the corner. To the left she could see the street as it climbed and curved up the hill. Around the corner on the hill she could see the white house with its large covered veranda with its view of the town and the Java Sea. Her house. The house that she and Matt had lived in for a year. She turned away and went back inside.

The place was furnished simply but cheerfully, and a large bouquet of gladioli graced the table. There was even a small refrigerator in the corner near the bathroom.

'It looks wonderful,' she said to Nicky. 'After spending two days eating and sleeping and sitting next to strangers in a confined space, this is heaven. I'm going to shower and drop, and you'll see me when you see me, which may be tomorrow or next week, who knows?'

'Ibu is cooking *nasi goreng istimewa* for dinner tonight,' Nicky said evenly.

'I'll be there at seven.'

Nicky laughed. 'I thought you might.'

Rae was too keyed-up to sleep. She showered and washed her hair and put on a cotton nightgown, and lay on the bed, exhausted, yet wide awake. She looked at her watch. Three-thirty in the afternoon, local time. It was four-thirty in the morning in New York, eleven hours earlier. She turned on her other side. Her body wouldn't hold still. Her brain wouldn't quit flashing images of Jason Grant, of eyes so blue they made her think of cloudless winter skies in the snowy mountains of Vermont, where the air was so cold and so pure that it tasted like champagne.

Sleep did not come. Finally, in frustration, she got up and started unpacking her suitcases, hanging her

clothes in the wardrobe and putting her teaching
materials in the bookcase. Carefully she unwrapped
Matt's picture in its silver frame and set it on the chest
of drawers. Warm brown eyes smiled into hers. Soft
sandy-coloured hair fell over his forehead. It never
would stay in place.

'Well, I made it,' she said to the picture. 'I'm back,
but it's not the same.'

She hadn't expected it to be the same, of course.
Three and a half years ago the two of them had arrived
in this town, excited about the wonderful opportunity
to live in the exotic Far East for two years. Life then
had seemed so full of adventure and hope, and they'd
enjoyed learning about the culture and the people.
Less than a year later, Matt had been forced out of his
contract and they'd returned to New York, vowing that
one day they would come back.

There was still a terrible sadness inside her, a sadness
she didn't think would ever go away, yet she could
think of him now without the sorrow clogging her
throat and tears burning her eyes.

After Matt's death she had thrown herself into her
studies, determined to get her master's degree in
teaching English as a Second Language, determined to
stay busy just so she wouldn't have time to feel the
pain, the aching loneliness of her empty life.

She lay back on the bed, her eyes on Matt's face,
and then, suddenly, she was alseep.

When she awoke she felt as if she'd been drugged. It
was dark around her. Her head swam, her eyes
wouldn't focus, her body felt numb. A strange noise
pounded in her ears. No, it wasn't strange altogether.

Tokay, tokay, tokay, tokay.

She strained her ears. Nothing. She took a deep
breath and closed her eyes. Maybe she could go back
to sleep.

Tokay, tokay, tokay.

She sat straight up in bed. A lizard, that was what it was. One of the bigger variety, by the sound of it. It seemed to come from the bathroom. She tried her legs, which didn't feel at all as if they would hold her up, but she made it to the bathroom anyway. She switched on the light and looked around. She discovered the reptile, some twelve inches of him, tail and all, clinging to the outside of the mosquito screen of the window. The glass louvres were open, which had done nothing to block the sound. They were also letting hot, humid air into the cool room.

'Thanks a lot for the welcome,' she said, bending closer to see. 'But you could have picked a better moment.'

The lizard stared coldly out of its beady eyes and said nothing. Rae glanced at her watch. It was a little after six. 'OK, so you did me a favour. Can't miss my *nasi goreng istimewa*. Now do me another favour and get lost. You're not too pretty to look at.' She flipped the louvres shut.

She dressed in a white cotton dress and brushed her hair. It looked a lot better—the short chestnut curls standing out in a fluffy mass around her head no longer resembled a dirty floor mop. She put on a little make-up and ventured out of her room in search of friends and dinner.

Jason Grant would be there, and this Anouk, whoever she was. Rae wondered who else would be there. From experience she knew that Nicky and David King's house was never empty. Nicky, gregarious and full of life, needed people around her. She loved giving parties and was always inviting people to stop by for coffee or a cold drink, at least in the afternoons when she was back from her photographic safaris or had finished working in her dark-room.

Rae heard voices out on the large veranda off the sitting-room and stepped outside through the open

french windows. She would have to get used again to
the early darkness. Day gave way to night at about six
in the evening every day of the year. There was a lamp
on the veranda, and a variety of candles, and Rae
could smell the familiar fragrance of mosquito coils.
She glanced around quickly, seeing Nicky and David,
and the American, Jason Grant, sitting in rattan chairs
nursing drinks. Anouk, whoever she was, was apparently otherwise engaged, or maybe Jason hadn't invited
her along.

'There you are!' Nicky called out. 'David, go and
pour her a drink.'

Obediently David dragged his gangling frame out of
his chair. Rae held up her hand. 'Just some water or
iced tea, please. I don't think I should subject my
system to alcohol just yet.'

She sat down in a chair, uncomfortably aware of
Jason's assessing blue eyes. Maybe he was just looking,
not assessing. She wondered why she felt so self-
conscious. He was a big, imposing man with wide
shoulders and thick, unruly dark hair. He radiated
competence and composure, but there was no reason
why she should feel the way she did.

'Did you sleep?' Nicky asked, and Rae said, yes, but
that she'd been awakened by a tokay, which made
Nicky laugh.

'Welcome back,' she said.

David returned, jauntily balancing above his head a
tray with a glass of iced tea, sliced lemon and a bowl of
sugar. With elaborate show he deposited it on a small
table next to Rae's chair.

Rae laughed. David had to make a show of everything. He was too thin to be handsome, but he made
up for it in personality.

Three more people showed up for drinks and dinner,
laughing, talking, and all in good cheer. Josie and
Steve brought pictures of their baby girl for Rae to see,

because it would probably be another day or so before she could get to the house to admire her in real life. They'd waited endless years for a child, and now she filled their entire life.

Rae was still groggy, and she said little as the others talked. Kurt Reinecker, the balding Bavarian she'd met earlier that afternoon, elaborated on the preparations for the annual Oktoberfest which the Germans in the community were putting on.

Jason seemed not to be the talkative sort. Rae gathered from the general conversation, however, that he worked on a government contract managing a credit project for small-scale enterprises. Something about loans and managerial assistance—she didn't quite catch the finer details, but apparently it was big and important. No doubt it was, she could tell by just looking at the man. He wasn't one who wasted his time on trivial matters.

All through the evening, she was increasingly aware of being observed by Jason Grant. It wasn't the standard type of attention a man paid to a woman. His interest had a different quality. She felt exposed under his blue gaze, as if she were some bug under a microscope. He didn't say a great deal, but he listened to every word she said. She felt self-conscious, and more and more irritated. What the hell was the matter with the man? Why was he watching her every move? Why was he listening to her as if it mattered to him what she said about her teaching job? He had nothing to do with her and she had nothing to do with him.

I'm tired, she said to herself. I'm just over-reacting. Aircraft fumes, jet lag, lack of sleep, what can you expect?

The *nasi goreng* was delicious, but she had little appetite. What she really needed was bed and sleep for the next three days.

'What's the matter with this Grant?' she asked Nicky

after everyone had left. 'Did you see him look at me? As if I were something that came crawling out from under a stone.'

Nicky laughed. 'Oh, Rae, come on, don't exaggerate. Jason is a nice guy.'

'Nice guy my foot! He doesn't like me.'

'He doesn't know you.'

'Right. So why was he so obnoxious?'

'He was not obnoxious.'

'He was, too.'

David gave a loud groan. 'Children, children, please stop squabbling.'

Nicky laughed. 'Tell her Jason is a nice guy.'

'Jason is a nice guy,' he said promptly.

'See?'

'Tell me why he doesn't like me,' Rae demanded, glaring at Nicky. 'I'm right, aren't I? There's something fishy and you don't want to tell me.'

Nicky yawned elaborately. 'How about if we talk about it tomorrow? I'm bushed.'

'I'm not asking you to do push-ups, for Pete's sake! Just tell me!'

'All right, all right.' Nicky gave a long-suffering sigh. 'Jason didn't want to hire you as a teacher, but he——'

'He didn't *what*?'

'He didn't think you were qualified enough because——'

Rae felt the heat of fury wash over her. 'I am a qualified elementary school teacher! On top of that I have my ESL degree. I am *quite* qualified! And what does it have to do with him? Who the hell is he? Is he on the school-board?'

'He is.'

'Oh, great,' she muttered. 'Does he have any kids in school?'

'Yes. A daughter. She'll be in first grade in September.'

Rae's heart sank. She closed her eyes. She hadn't even started the job yet and already she had an enemy. No wonder she'd felt uncomfortable. It hadn't, after all, been her imagination. He had indeed been scrutinising her all evening.

She took a deep breath. 'So why am I here, if the lord and master didn't want me?'

Nicky's green eyes gleamed. 'He was outvoted. Five against one.'

'And he accepted that?'

'Now don't be nasty, Rae.'

'I feel nasty. All evening he stares holes in me; I've got the right to be nasty. So why does he think I'm not qualified enough?'

'He wanted somebody older and more experienced. You've never actually taught ESL. This is your first job.'

'But I've taught kids for five years, including a year right here in this school! That should count for something. I knew exactly what I was getting myself into.'

'That's why I tried my darndest to get you back here. And everybody else on the board and all the other parents are happy to have you.'

'That's a relief, at least.' Rae shifted in her chair. 'I could use a drink. A real one.'

SICO, the Semarang International Civic Organisation—its acronym not arrived at by coincidence—had organised a welcome party for Rae, which was to be held at the Kelly house. Josie and Steve lived in the Kelly house. No matter who lived in the house, it was called the Kelly house. Big parties were always at the Kelly house because, among the expatriate houses, it was the best place for parties. It had a huge room for dancing and an enormous lawn for standing around and talking. Rae remembered that she and Matt had attended a New Year's party at the Kelly house, a week after Steve and Josie had moved in. The SICO representatives had arrived at the door, introduced themselves, offered help, and then told the new occupants that there was going to be a party at their house.

'Oh,' Josie had said.

'We always have it in this house.'

'Oh, well, in that case. . .'

And so, year after year, the parties continued at the house, no matter who lived in it. It was a duty that came with living in the house. You got the house, you got the parties.

Rae scrutinised herself in the mirror as she got ready for the party. It was the third dress she had tried on, a slinky teal affair with narrow shoulder-straps. She wondered why it was suddenly so important to look just right. She hadn't cared for a long time now what men thought of her, how she looked. It hadn't mattered.

So why are you making such a fuss? she asked herself. You look fine.

Maybe the cream dress is better.

This one is fine. Leave it on. Fix your face.

She made up her face, taking twice as long as she did normally.

There was a knock on her door. It was Nicky, dressed in loose harem trousers and an embroidered tunic in vivid fuchsia. A twig of bougainvillaea blooms of the same colour was tucked into the blonde curls on top of her head. 'Are you ready to go?' she asked.

Rae stared despairingly at her reflection in the mirror. 'I don't know.'

'What do you mean, you don't know? You look gorgeous. What's the matter?'

'My hair.'

'What of it?'

'It's all over the place!'

Nicky laughed. 'It's supposed to be all over the place.' She gave Rae a knowing look. 'Are you nervous?'

'Why would I be nervous?'

Nicky shrugged, green eyes innocent. 'Beats me.' She put her hand on the doorknob. 'Let's go.'

As they entered the gate of the Kelly house, Rae couldn't help feeling a sense of anticipation, or was it trepidation? Coloured lights were strung between the trees. Small tables were set out on the grass, illuminated by candles. There was music and the sounds of people talking and laughing.

Soon Rae was among them, getting hugged and kissed by old friends and welcomed by strangers who all smiled at her and shook her hand. She was rather glorying in all the attention, feeling a sense of homecoming. At the large university she had felt lost among the thousands of students; here everybody knew who she was, even before she'd met them.

Josie drew her away and practically dragged her up the stairs to the nursery. 'She's asleep,' she whispered, 'but I want you to see her.'

'I'm sorry I didn't come by yesterday afternoon,' Rae whispered back. 'I fell asleep. I've been so tired.'

'Sure, I know.'

A night-light glowed on the far wall. Rae admired the peacefully sleeping baby, the tiny nose, the puckered mouth, the soft blonde curls. I could have had one like that by now, she thought, feeling a swift flash of pain. 'She looks like an angel,' she said softly. 'I can't imagine how she's sleeping through all this noise.'

Downstairs, more people had arrived. Rae went to the bar for a drink, joking with Josie's husband, Steve, who filled her glass with vermouth and soda.

'Hello, Rae.' The deep, vibrant voice was familiar.

She turned around. Drink in hand, Jason gave her

his cool, polite smile and she felt an odd quivering in her stomach as she looked at him. There was something about the man that threw her off balance, and she didn't like the feeling.

'Hello,' she returned.

'Quite a place, this,' he said.

'Yes. Excuse me, please.' She moved past him, away from him, not caring whether she was polite or not. In her haste she almost ran into a broad, bulky frame, and an arm reached out and swung her sideways.

'What's the hurry? Don't you want to say hello?'

She felt a jolt of happy surprise. 'Kevin!' She hugged him and he kissed her on both cheeks.

'I was looking for you,' he said with a grin. 'I'd have come to see you sooner, but I was in Jakarta battling the bureaucrats. I just came back this afternoon. So how are you?' Grey eyes looked at her appreciatively. 'You look smashing, love.'

She loved his cocky Aussie accent, and felt a warm glow of delight at seeing him again. He'd been a good friend when she and Matt had lived in Semarang before. He was in his early thirties and still happily single, or so he had said in his last Christmas card to her. A disastrous marriage had put him off matrimony for ever, or so he claimed.

'Thank you. And I'm fine,' she said. 'So, are you still building roads and bridges and aqueducts and whatnot?'

He rolled his eyes. 'We try.' He took her hand. 'Come along and I'll introduce you to some friends of mine.'

It was strange to see so many unfamiliar faces. Two and a half years had seen a great turnover of expats. With projects and jobs finished, people moved on to other assignments in other countries. New projects and contracts brought in new people. The Indonesians were serious about improving their economy and developing their industries: fisheries, textiles, rattan furniture, engineering, and foreign experts and consultants were invited to help do the job.

Rae enjoyed getting to know the people and talking with them about the school and their children. Everyone was pleased to have her, and many invited her over for tea, drinks, dinner. Did she want to join SICC, the Semarang International Cooking Club? Did she want to come to exercise classes? Did she want to go running with the Hash House Harriers every Monday afternoon at four? It was what she had enjoyed before, the easy friendship among the people, the closeness of a group that depended on each other for almost everything—schooling, entertainment, food orders, books to read, help and support in case of problems.

She met Susan Thompson, the school's diminutive British principal, who introduced her to Hillie Moerman, the mother of two of her new students, Sander and Miranda. Hillie had bright, laughing blue eyes and a smiling mouth, and wore an outlandish outfit with tigers jumping all over it. She was slim and tall, with soft wavy hair the colour of honey in a flattering short cut. She warned Rae not to put up with any nonsense from her twosome. She had two more at home, she said, four-year-old twin boys, and as far as she was concerned the only way to deal with children was with a strict but loving hand. She hoped Rae had a couple of those. Rae took an instant liking to the woman. She had a nice sense of humour and an infectious laugh. Her eyes brightened when Jason joined them.

'Where's Joost?' he asked.

'Talking business somewhere in a corner. My husband the workaholic. He hates parties, you know that. How's Anouk's ankle?'

'It's better now.' He grimaced. 'You know my

daughter. She doesn't have the patience to be an invalid.'

'Have you met?' Susan Thompson asked, looking from Jason to Rae.

'We have,' Jason answered.

Susan smiled at Rae. 'Jason's daughter will be one of your students.'

Surprised, Rae glanced over at Jason. 'I'm teaching ESL.'

'She doesn't speak English.' He smiled crookedly at her confusion. 'Her mother was Dutch and all we spoke at home was Dutch. The two of us still do.'

Was his wife dead? For a moment Rae forgot everything, feeling a stirring of pity, for him, for the little girl she didn't know.

'You don't speak English to her at all?'

'No.' He did not elaborate. It seemed to Rae a strange situation.

'She'll learn quickly,' she said. 'They all do at that age.'

'Six months and they're virtually fluent,' Susan added.

'I'm not so sure,' he said drily.

Rae couldn't help thinking that something strange was going on, but she had no idea what. Was he challenging her, the new teacher?

He looked at the empty glass in her hand. 'Can I get you another drink?'

'No, thank you.'

Several people joined them, engaging Jason in conversation about his work, and Rae escaped. He found her again, a while later as she was standing in the room looking at an exotic Bali painting full of wild creatures with bug eyes and wings.

'Have you ever been to Bali?' he asked.

'No.' She stared at the painting, not wanting to look at him.

'S...

Josie a place, as long as you stay away from the

We just got it ... side. 'You like the painting?

Bali. It's so weird, ... months ago when we went to

and keep finding other ... ou can just stand there

that monkey?' ... ok here, do you see

Other people gathered arou... followed on the Balinese culture, so ... a discussion rest of Indonesia. Rae managed to slip ... from the moved out into the garden where people we... ay, and around in chairs and on the veranda steps. Mosquito coils glowed bravely in the dark. She wandered away into the warm darkness, away from the music and the people. Looking up, she saw the moon through the palm fronds, and the silver glittering of faraway stars.

Crickets chirped in a cheerful chorus in the grass and she listened to the sounds, feeling peace settle inside her. Then there was another sound, the sound of quiet steps in the grass.

'Are you avoiding me?' Jason's voice. She turned to face him, stiffening with resentment. She didn't want him here in the quiet of the night, disturbing her peace. But it was too late already.

'You want the truth, or shall I be polite?'

His mouth quirked. 'By all means, the truth, please.'

'Well, yes, as a matter of fact, I am avoiding you.'

'Why?'

'You make me uncomfortable.'

He raised his brows, looking puzzled. 'You are direct, aren't you?'

'It makes life a lot less complicated.'

He put his hands in his pockets. 'Why do I make you uncomfortable?' he asked, frowning.

She straightened herself to her full height, which didn't amount to much at five feet four inches,

better
especially not next to him, but j̶ don't have
anyway. 'You're scrutinising m̶
to explain it to you.'   right now. This is a
'I would like to talk to being interrogated.'
'I don't feel like talk̶rama,' he mocked.
party. I'm not in the̶
He laughed. 'A̶ ̶ark. 'Excuse me,' she said again,
She ignored ̶i him, but this time he didn't let her
turning awa̶gripped her wrist.
go. His h̶Rae, don't go.'
'Pleas̶'
She ̶̶opped, looking at him silently. His face was
ser̶̶us and he let go of her wrist.

'You will be my daughter's teacher,' he said quietly.
'I think it's important we get along, if only for her
sake.'

'I certainly would prefer that,' she said coolly.

'I'm sorry if I made you uncomfortable.'

She wasn't sure if he was or not, but she nodded. 'I
hope that as a teacher I will live up to your
expectations.'

He raised his eyebrows. 'Which are?'

'I don't know, but you have some, and you're not at
all sure I will do. Isn't that right?' She looked right at
him.

He frowned. 'So, you heard.' It was a statement, not
a question. He had voted against hiring her and he
knew that she knew.

'Everybody knows everything here, you know that,'
she said.

He sighed, his expression one of irritation and
impatience. 'Yes.' He took a swallow from his drink
and studied her for a moment. She didn't look away
and a faint smile crept around his lips.

'Anouk, my daughter, has a bad sprain; that's why I
didn't bring her to dinner on Thursday,' he said. 'But I
would like her to meet you before school starts. I

mee...

The h... if you'd come by my house and
hide it behi..it ...
to meet her, too. ...ed her, but she managed to
won't be so threaten...ional teacher smile. 'I'd like
His mouth quirked. ...er own surroundings she
How about tomorrow? Abou... teacher.'
Dutch style.' ...n't threaten easily.
'That sounds nice. Four will be fine. ...We'll have tea,
live?' ...re do you
'From Nicky and David's, just follow th... road
around the corner, to the third house on the right. The
house on the hill.'

The house on the hill. She felt her heart contract. It
can't be your house, she thought stupidly. The house
on the hill was mine and Matt's. You can't be living
there.

But of course he could. The house was rented,
furniture and all, by foreign companies for their
employees to live in.

'Something wrong?' Jason asked, looking at her,
eyebrows raised, and she shook her head and swallowed hard. It seemed suddenly so much warmer.

'No, no. I'll find it. No problem at all.'

'Why didn't you tell me Jason lived in my old house?'
Rae asked Nicky after they came home from the party.

Nicky poured herself a glass of boiled water from a
bottle in the refrigerator. 'I'm sorry,' she said. 'I didn't
think about it. The Grahams lived in it after you left,
and. . .' She shrugged. 'I'm sorry, Rae, really.'

Rae sighed. 'It's just a house, I know.' She bit her
lip. 'He asked me to drop by tomorrow to meet his
daughter.'

Nicky groaned. 'Will it bother you to go there?'

Rae shrugged. 'It will be strange to see somebody

of course,
else living there. I knew the ntal slob. No
but. . .anyway, I'm just being get it.'
sense in making it a great about the house,
She went to bed, Matt's chair, showering
thinking about Jason their bed.
in their shower, sl ought. What do you care who
This is insane You didn't own it. You didn't pick
lives in that p'; you didn't even *like* most of it.
out the furation came that if a German or English
The r ith one or two kids and a dog were living in it
couple now, she wouldn't have cared half as much. It made a
difference that it was Jason Grant who lived there now.
Jason Grant who made her uncomfortable, whose blue
eyes stirred something inside her. Something frightening and exciting. Something she didn't want to feel at
all.

CHAPTER TWO

EVERYTHING drooped over the ga.... same. The bougainvillaea just as it had a few years ....ing a passionate pink, mango tree still cast its shade ove huge, spreading house. Rae would have to go to the front of the the bell, not go around to the back where she'd always entered through the kitchen.

A small Indonesian woman opened the door. She was dressed in the traditional clothes: a fitted top and thin jacket over a sarong wrapped around her waist. Her greying hair was tied back in a knot and she was barefoot.

Rae smiled at her. '*Pak Grant ada?* Is Mr Grant here?' she asked.

The woman smiled and nodded. Two of her top front teeth were a shining silver. '*Ada.*'

She led Rae into the house, through the living-room to the veranda. Nothing had changed. The furniture was still the same, rattan chairs and sofa with cushions covered with batik upholstery fabric. On the veranda even the birdcage was still there.

'Please sit down,' the woman said in Indonesian. 'I will tell Pak Grant you are here.'

But there was no need for that. He was there right behind her, dressed casually in khaki trousers and a blue short-sleeved shirt that showed muscled brown arms.

'I thought I heard you,' he said, taking one of the other seats. 'Anouk will be here in a minute. I'm glad you could come.'

27

'My social calendar isn't very full yet,' she _____.
he laughed.

'It won't take long. There's always pick up again.
It's a little quiet just now, with a _ed in Semarang
home-leave, but in September ___
Well, I suppose you know. I was here for less than
before, didn't you?'

'Yes. I taught at
a year, though_me back on to the veranda, carrying a
The wor which she put down on the table. Jason
loaded _y at her. '_Dank u wel_,' he said.
nod_ed

'Don't tell me,' Rae said, 'that your cook speaks
Dutch.'

'She does. Sauda is pre-independence vintage.
During the colonial times Dutch was the official
language.'

Yes, of course, Rae remembered that now. She
heard a noise and, turning around, she saw a little girl
with flaming red hair gathered in two curly pigtails. She
leaned against the door, face mutinous.

'Come and sit with us, Anouk,' Jason said in English,
and the girl hopped over on one leg and sat down. She
wore bright green shorts and a white shirt, and her left
ankle was wrapped in an elastic bandage. She looked
wiry and thin, and her legs were covered with scratches
and bruises.

'My daughter Anouk,' Jason said to Rae. 'Anouk,
this is Mrs Smith. She'll teach you English when you
start first grade in a couple of weeks.' He spoke to his
daughter in English and Rae watched the girl.

The pale face flushed. Rebellious grey eyes glared at
Rae. You just try, the eyes said.

Great, Rae thought. Just what I need first thing: a
problem case. She had no intention, however, of letting
the little thing get to her. She smiled her most confident
smile. 'We'll have fun. You'll learn quickly.'

You've got to be kidding, the eyes signalled.

She may not speak English, Rae thought, but she certainly understands it.

Jason poured three cups of tea, adding sugar and a generous measure of milk to the one he gave to Anouk.

Rae added a little sugar to the cup he handed her and took a small sip. It was very hot. She was aware of the tension hovering in the air.

'How did you sprain your ankle?' Rae asked, pointing at the girl's ankle and raising her brows in question.

The girl pretended not to hear.

'Anouk!' Jason's voice threatened.

''K ben uit de boom gevallen,' she muttered, staring stonily into her tea.

'She fell out of a tree,' Jason translated. His mouth quirked. 'Trying to get to the guavas before the boys next door did,' he added.

The tea was hot and strong. Rae added some milk. 'What makes this Dutch tea?' she asked, searching desperately for a neutral subject of discussion.

'Tea in the afternoon is always a break, never a meal.' There was a gleam of humour in his eyes. 'And only children drink it with milk.'

'Well, I guess I blew that one.'

'You're forgiven.'

Anouk leaned over and made a grab for the biscuits on the table. Jason said something sharp in Dutch, and she picked up the plate and offered it to Rae, eyes defiant.

'They look good,' Rae said, taking one. 'Did you help make them?'

The girl said nothing.

'Answer the question,' Jason said curtly.

She tilted her chin. *'Ja,'* she said.

Something flickered in Jason's eyes, as if he was ready to say something else, but he was silent. Something was going on, there was no doubt about that.

Rae looked again at Anouk's small, thin face, feeling a rush of pity. She was staring in her tea now, her shoulders hunched. Her thin legs dangled over the edge of the chair, feet not touching the ground. Six years was not very old, not nearly old enough to do without a mother. Not old enough to carry so much pain and anger—it was all there in the face, the posture, the rebellion in her eyes.

Anouk took the cup with two hands and drank the milky liquid down in a few large gulps. She straightened and put the cup and saucer on the table, saying something in Dutch to her father. He answered her, apparently excusing her, for she left the veranda and went inside.

'I must apologise for my daughter's behaviour,' Jason said. 'She's not normally so rude.'

'She wasn't happy about meeting me, and she didn't know how to handle it. It's all right.'

'It's not all right.' He frowned. 'I hope she will not be a problem for you.'

'I'll handle it, don't worry.'

He gave her a speculative look, as if he wasn't at all sure about that, then picked up the teapot. 'More tea?'

She nodded. 'Tell me, why didn't you teach her English and Dutch at the same time?'

'My wife was adamant that she learn Dutch. We didn't think English would be any problem, since we would be living in the States or abroad and most likely not in Holland for any length of time.' He shrugged. 'If we didn't try to teach her Dutch when she was young, she would never learn. All my wife's family live in Holland, her parents, her brother and sister. She didn't want Anouk to feel a foreigner with her own grandparents and aunts and uncles.'

'No, I can understand that.' Rae frowned. 'Why hasn't she learned English yet? She's six now?'

'She was little when we lived in New York and she

spoke some English, but not much. Three years ago—
a little less, actually—we moved to Holland. We were
going to be there just for a year; I was teaching.' He
paused. 'Then my wife died.' His voice was even, but
she could tell that it took an effort for him to say the
words. 'It was easier and better to stay on and teach
for another year. We lived with my parents-in-law,
which was a blessing, especially for Anouk.'

He drained his cup and leaned back in his chair.
'Then I was offered this job and decided to come here.
Teaching wasn't what I meant to do, and we couldn't
stay on in Holland forever. We needed to make our
own life, so here we are.'

'What if you speak English to her at home?'

'Strange as that may seem to you, it doesn't feel
right. It seems forced and unnatural. Dutch is what we
always spoke together; it's our family language, even
though it is not my mother tongue. But I have tried, of
course, and she rebels. She'll only answer in Dutch.'

'Maybe it'll be easier once she's in school.'

'I hope so.'

Rae looked at the birdcage, listening to the twitters
of the tiny birds.

'Do you like this house?' she asked on impulse, and
he shrugged.

'It's a house. I like this veranda, though. At night I
sit here and read. Very relaxing.'

'Yes.' That was what she and Matt used to do. 'Do
you hear a flautist some time? From the Kampong?'
She gestured to the left where small houses clustered
below at the bottom of the hill.

He gave her an odd look. 'Yes. How do you know?'

'I used to live here with my husband.' There was no
reason not to tell him. It was a simple fact, and he
would hear it from somebody sooner or later.

He stared at her. 'In this house?'

She gave a half smile. 'Yes. It seems. . .strange to be sitting here again.'

He frowned slightly, still looking at her. 'I understand now,' he said, 'why you had that look on your face yesterday when I told you how to get here.' He paused. 'I'm sorry. I hope it isn't painful to be here. Nicky told me your husband died.'

'Yes, two years ago.'

There was a silence, a silence full of strange vibrations and feelings.

'My wife died almost two years ago as well,' he said quietly, holding her gaze. His blue eyes mirrored pain and sorrow, a reflection of her own.

She swallowed. She was aware of her heart beating, of blood flowing through her veins, of her nerves tingling.

She wanted to ask him if he had loved his wife, as she had loved Matt. If he had wanted to die too, when she had died; if he had felt the coldness of the effort not to feel, not to cry, not ever to feel again. But of course she could not ask him any of these questions. He was a stranger, a man she had only met a few days earlier.

'I'm sorry,' she said, feeling inadequate. She thought of his little red-headed daughter, and again pity filled her heart. I'll have to try to reach her, she thought.

She stood up slowly, straightening her skirt. 'I'd better go now. Thank you for the tea.'

'I appreciate your coming.' He came to his feet and stood close to her, so tall next to her five feet four. She was acutely aware of him, every nerve registering his proximity. The feeling unnerved her. He moved aside, to the door, and she followed him into the living-room.

Once this had been her living-room, but she no longer belonged here. Now she was a stranger in this house and this man would sleep in her bed tonight.

'Do you mind if I leave through the back door?' she asked on impulse, and he turned to look at her.

'No, of course not, if you like.'

In the kitchen, Sauda was chopping some ginger root. She smiled at Rae and wished her goodbye. Rae followed Jason out of the door and down the drive. He opened the heavy gates for her. She was uncomfortably aware of his eyes as she walked down the street, wondering what he thought of her and what he was expecting of her as a teacher.

The following days she was busy at the school, organising her classroom, talking to Susan Thompson and the other teachers, and searching around town for additional materials. Only one more week before school started. She was anxious to begin, although she was apprehensive about the problem with Jason's daughter. She fervently hoped she could help Anouk and prove to Jason that she was a competent teacher. She felt a nervous twittering in her stomach every time she thought of Jason Grant, and it annoyed her.

'Oh, damn!' she muttered to herself. 'What am I getting myself into now?'

Fortunately, Kevin provided some diversion. They had an elaborate Chinese dinner at the Mandarin restaurant, and went to the pictures another night, sitting in a room full of smoke from the smelly clove cigarettes.

Kevin told her he was giving a birthday party and asked if she would give him a hand with the planning, which she was glad to be able to do.

'I'll bake you a birthday cake, too, if you want one.'

He grinned. 'I was hoping you'd say that. We've all missed your birthday cakes. That's the real reason they wanted you back here, but nobody would admit that, of course.'

Rae laughed. Cake decorating was just a hobby now,

but while she'd been in high school she had earned
money for college working in a bakery during summer
vacations. 'How would you like me to decorate it? Not
with roses or racing cars, I assume?'

'I'll leave it to you. Be as creative as you like.'

Being creative was what she liked; her classroom,
too, was evidence of that. She wanted it to be a happy,
cheerful place for her students, who no doubt would
feel anxious and apprehensive about a teacher who
could not speak their language and would not understand them.

The first day of school arrived and the children were
brought in by their parents: a tiny Japanese girl, a
French-speaking Belgian boy, Sander and Miranda
Moerman, a German-speaking Swiss boy, and Anouk.
Rae woud teach them for the first half of the morning,
after which they would go back to their regular class-
rooms. For the second part of the day she would teach
four other students.

Anouk arrived, dressed in a blue and white dress
and sturdy blue sandals, delivered by Jason.

'Good morning.' Rae smiled confidently, but her
chest tightened at the sight of him. In his crisp white
shirt, he looked energetic and charged for a new day's
work. His black hair was freshly combed, but looked
ready to do its own thing without notice. Anouk stood
woodenly at the door, as if she had no intention of
entering. Jason bent down, kissed his daughter's cheek
and told her something in Dutch, to which she did not
reply. He straightened and looked at Rae. 'I'll give her
a while to get settled and then I'll talk to you.'

Rae nodded. You'll give me a while, you mean, she
said silently. She watched him go, seeing him jump
lithely into a battered Toyota Landcruiser and drive
off. He drove his own car. Most people here had
drivers. She looked back at Anouk, who hadn't stirred.

She touched the girl's shoulder. 'Let's go inside. I'll show you your desk.' Reluctantly the girl moved.

'This is your desk,' Rae said. 'Desk,' she repeated, putting her hand flat on the blue-painted table. She touched the chair. 'Chair.'

Anouk ignored her and sat down. Rae left her and moved on to the little Japanese girl, who sat frozen in her chair with silent tears streaming down her face.

This first morning was spent mostly getting to know the children and making them comfortable in her classroom. They played some easy games. Anouk participated, whispering in Dutch to the two Moerman children. The three of them laughed and giggled among themselves. It was unfortunate to have three of them speaking the same language, but this first day she let them go ahead.

There was snack-time and then recess, and Rae watched the children play outside. Anouk, bright-eyed and confident, was taking charge of the games. In the playground she was a different child from the angry, defiant girl whom Rae saw in her classroom.

'So how was your first day?' Nicky asked when Rae came home from school a little after one. School started early in the morning as the afternoons were too hot for anyone to concentrate, and air-conditioning was too expensive for the moment.

Rae told her about the tiny Japanese girl, who'd looked desperately unhappy the whole morning, and about Anouk, whose hostile attitude did not show great promise.

'She wasn't so happy coming here,' Nicky said, 'but I've never been able to talk to her. She pretends she doesn't know English. If you ask me, she understands a lot.'

'That's what I thought.'

'Well, give her some time. Maybe she'll turn around after a while. You know how kids are.'

For some reason Rae wasn't so sure. There was something very tough and stubborn about the little girl. She took a drink of iced tea. 'So, tell me about your morning,' she said to Nicky.

'I went to the *pasar*, to the meat and fish section. There was a great collection of flies there this morning.'

Rae made a face. 'You are such a pervert, Nicky.'

Nicky laughed. 'Artistic talent, that's what it's called.'

Nicky had a rather bizarre way of looking at the world. She had a collection of pictures of feet: bare feet, clean, dirty, callused; feet with shoes, shiny shoes, worn-out shoes, dusty shoes. 'You can analyse an entire country just by looking at the citizens' feet,' she'd proclaimed.

Nicky swallowed the last of her iced tea. 'Listen, we're planning a weekend in Sarangan, a group of us. It's gorgeous up in the mountains. Heavenly cool. It's one of those former colonial hill stations, that's what the British called them. I don't know what the Dutch here called them.'

Rae nodded. 'I've heard of it. It's on the western half of the island, isn't it? You wrote to me about it last year.'

'It's a magnificent drive out there,' Nicky said, her voice taking on an overdramatic quality. 'It's wild and primitive with deep, dark forests and steep hills and hairpin turns. It's wonderful.' She sighed ecstatically.

'As long as some goat doesn't make you drive off the road and down the cliffs,' Rae said drily. 'I wouldn't miss it for the world. What weekend?'

'The first or second weekend after the Oktoberfest, I can't remember. I'll look it up.'

Rae thoroughly enjoyed the teaching. The children were all bright and eager to learn, with the exception of Anouk who showed nothing but resistance, ignoring any attempt Rae made to draw her out. Two weeks later there was no progress whatsoever.

On Friday at recess Rae held Anouk back in the classroom. 'Anouk,' she said gently, 'I want to talk to you.' She put an arm around the thin shoulders, feeling the small body stiffen in response. 'I think you know a lot of English. I think you can understand everything, or almost everything I am saying to you. Am I right?'

No response. The grey eyes stared stonily at the desk-top.

'I would like to be your friend,' Rae went on. 'I would like to help you with your English so you can do your schoolwork. It is very important to do your schoolwork.' She paused, but there was still no reaction. 'Anouk, I know there is a reason why you don't want to speak English. Can you tell me what it is? Is there a problem? I really would like to help.'

Anouk sat unmoving in her chair. She might as well have been a statue. Rae gently squeezed the girl's shoulders. 'Let's try, all right?' She stood up. 'You can go and play now.'

Head held high, Anouk walked out of the door, not looking at Rae. With a sigh Rae watched her go. Her words had obviously been wasted.

Rae talked to Ann Rosen, Anouk's regular classroom teacher. She had not heard a word of English out of Anouk. However, the girl did all her work: writing numbers and letters, filling out worksheets involving pictures, playing games, drawing pictures. 'Let's give her some more time,' she suggested.

Every morning Jason dropped his daughter off at school, wishing Rae a polite good morning before driving off in the battered Landcruiser or sometimes in a white Toyota sedan. It made her apprehensive to see him coming, wondering when he was going to demand a report. At the end of the third week she decided to

take the initiative. Anouk was inside talking to the
Moerman children, paying no attention to her father.

'I'm afraid it's not going well,' she said to Jason.
'Anouk has no interest at all in speaking English.'

His jaw hardened and his eyes narrowed. 'She has to
learn.'

'Is there any reason why she is resisting?'

'Nothing that I can think of.' He sounded flat and
impatient.

'I think we should talk. Maybe we can think of a
game plan.'

He frowned darkly. 'You're the teacher.'

She felt anger swell inside her. 'And you're her
father!' She was a teacher and she should have all the
answers: was that the way he saw it? There was a
problem and Daddy didn't want to hear about it. She
glared at him furiously, then turned and left him
standing at the school gate, not waiting for an answer.

All right, she would not ask for his co-operation
again. She would give it another week and see if
Anouk's attitude changed. If not, she would think of
something else.

Anouk was tougher than nails. Nothing could per-
suade her to utter a word in English. When another
week had passed without any progress, Rae decided to
try another angle. She stopped all efforts to make
Anouk talk, asking her no more questions, demanding
nothing of her, giving her only the most necessary
instructions. Without pressure, resistance was not necessary. Maybe on her own Anouk would come to the
conclusion she was missing out on something by not
participating.

There was some confusion at first, then Anouk went
over to the attack. She began to annoy the other
children, drawing attention to herself. When it got out
of hand, Rae took her desk and chair and moved her
away from the other students. 'Here are toys and books

and paper,' she said quietly. 'You may play and read or write, whatever you like. When you feel ready to behave yourself, you may join us again. We want you to be part of our class, but only if you do the work and follow the rules.' Anouk stared at her with rebellious grey eyes. There was no doubt she understood perfectly, but she gave no reply.

A week later Anouk was still sitting by herself. Rae marvelled at her tenacity. Once more she tried to have a calm and quiet talk with her. Again, nothing but silence and no response.

'I'd like a word with you,' Jason said one morning, and Rae stepped out of the classroom, her heart racing nervously. Why was she intimidated by this man? What was the matter with her? At night she thought of him, wondering if he was sitting out on the veranda listening to the flute player, or standing in that ridiculous green-tilted sunken bath, taking a shower. Or sleeping in the big bed. She kept thinking of his hands, tanned and strong with long, lean fingers.

'Anouk tells me you're not teaching her anything,' he said, the deep voice holding a hint of accusation. 'She's sitting by herself and you're not talking to her.'

'That's correct.' She looked right into the cool blue eyes. 'I told her as soon as she can behave herself and feels like participating, she is welcome to join us. It's up to her.'

Anger flared in his eyes. 'No,' he said slowly, 'it's up to you. *You* are the teacher. We hired you to teach the children English. It's been several weeks now and my daughter doesn't speak a word of English.'

Nerves jumped around in her stomach. He was blaming her. 'I know,' she said. 'But I've told you, it's not an educational problem. She refuses point-blank to learn.'

'And you don't have ways of handling that?'

'Do you?'

Something flickered in his eyes. 'I'm not a teacher.'

And she was, he meant. She should know how to deal with this child. She took a deep breath.

'I can teach a child, but only if he or she is willing to learn. You know we are not dealing with a normal situation here,' she said carefully.

The blue eyes narrowed dangerously. 'There is nothing abnormal about the situation,' he said coldly. 'She's six years old, does not speak English, and she needs to learn. You were hired specifically to teach English. It's as simple as that.'

Rae wanted to stay calm and in control, but it took all her strength not to turn her back on the arrogant face. She straightened her shoulders. 'Anouk is very intelligent and bright, probably even more than we give her credit for. She's been here for eight months and she speaks almost perfect Indonesian, or so I'm told. If she can learn Indonesian, she can learn English, but only——'

'Then I suggest you teach her.' Blue eyes looked at her coolly.

She clenched her teeth so hard that her jaws hurt. 'It's not a matter of whether I'm capable of teaching her English. It's a matter of her wanting to learn. And she doesn't; she has systematically refused.'

'Then motivate her, encourage her, give her incentives. All teaching skills, aren't they?' His condescending tone infuriated her. How dared he talk to her like that? Who did he think he was to insinuate that she didn't know her job? She took a deep breath in a last-ditch effort not to blow her cool.

'Your daughter does not wish to be motivated,' she said with admirable control. 'We have a problem on our hands and it's not merely an educational one. *You* are her father, so I suggest you figure out what it is, and then I am more than willing to help if I can.' She turned, her legs shaking, and walked back into her classroom.

Damn his arrogance! Damn his presumptuous attitude!

The run-in with him ruined her day; she couldn't get the incident out of her head. Nicky's green eyes looked at her searchingly when she came home a little after one.

'What's wrong with you?'

Rae sat down and told her, drinking a glass of iced tea and eating a shrimp salad which Ibu had prepared for their lunch.

Nicky frowned. 'I can't think what's got into him. He's not like that, you know. I've never known him to be anything but friendly and relaxed.'

'He's certainly not friendly and relaxed with me. He seems to think that since I'm the teacher I should straighten out his daughter for him. Thank God it's Friday. With a little luck I won't see him again till Monday.'

No such luck. It was a decided misfortune that she should run into him at Kevin's birthday party the next day. She'd spent all day on Saturday helping organise the food and baking a huge birthday cake. She'd decorated it with a picture of a bridge lined with thirty-two tiny candles, and palm trees in the background.

Kevin looked at the result and grinned. He put his arm around her shoulder and kissed her cheek. 'It's a masterpiece, love. Your bridge looks a lot more solid than the one we're building at the moment. The concrete is about as substantial as sugar frosting.'

Rae's good cheer went right out of the window when she saw Jason come into the room. It didn't take long before he had zeroed in on her.

'You have a definite talent with birthday cakes,' he said evenly.

And none with teaching, you mean, she tagged on in

thought. 'Thank you,' she said coolly. She took a sip from her drink, seeing his eyes skim discreetly over her body in the long green dress. She wondered why she felt so exposed under his casual gaze—or maybe it wasn't so casual.

'You don't look much like a teacher,' he said, with a barely perceptible smile.

She looked at him coldly. 'I'm sorry you don't approve.'

'Oh, I approve,' he said slowly. 'But it always amazes me what a difference clothes and make-up can make.'

She wasn't going to stand here and chat with him. 'If you'll excuse me, I'll——'

'No, I won't,' he said calmly. 'I believe we have a discussion to finish. You walked out on me at school yesterday.'

'I don't argue with parents in front of the students.'

'Very commendable. I suggest we discuss it now. No children here.'

'Not so very long ago I suggested we have a parent-teacher conference, and, if you remember correctly, you were not interested. Apparently you did not find it necessary to figure out what you can do to help your daughter.'

Anger leaped into his eyes. 'Are you insinuating that I'm not a good father?'

'I am saying that you didn't find it necessary to talk to me about your daughter.'

'I find it necessary now.'

She gritted her teeth. 'I am not available right now. This is a party. I am not working. I am trying to enjoy myself. Now, if you'll excuse me?' She walked out of the open doors into the garden, which was a big mistake. He was right behind her, cornering her between the veranda railing and the potted palms.

'I'm sorry to be such an inconvenience,' he said

coldly, 'but all I want is a few minutes. As for parent-teacher conferences, we can have one right here. We're not very formal here in Semarang, as you may have noticed.'

She wasn't going to get away from him here unless she pushed him bodily out of her way, which was not a realistic possibility. Her only choice was to talk to him and get it over with.

'I have no desire to waste my time arguing with you,' she said, 'so come to the point. Have you figured out why Anouk is behaving the way she is?'

'Obviously she's not happy in your classroom.'

Was that an accusation? It certainly sounded like one. She controlled her anger with an effort. 'She certainly isn't, but my classroom and what happens in it is not the reason and you know it. She'd made up her mind not to learn English way before she entered my classroom.'

'You must have come across other difficult children,' he stated. He pushed his hands in his pockets and waited for a reply.

'I have.' Her nerves were jumping. He looked very handsome in the shadowed darkness. Handsome and big and intimidating. She resented the fact that this man had such an impact on her emotions, her thoughts.

'I want this nonsense to stop,' he said coldly, as if by ordering it it would simply happen. It occurred to her that he was a man used to getting his way, making things happen if necessary. She felt a sudden admiration for Anouk, who dared defy her father, and it gave her, in some perverse way, a sense of satisfaction that he was being defeated by this scrap of a girl with freckles and red hair.

He frowned irritably when she remained silent. 'I want this nonsense to stop,' he repeated. 'I want her to learn. So what do you suggest we do?'

She shook her head. 'It's not nonsense, you know

that. Something else is going on, and perhaps you
understand it better than I do.'

'I don't understand what you're talking about.'

She forced the anger down. Did he think she was
stupid, or what? She willed her voice to stay calm.

'You know your daughter better than I do. You
knew there was going to be a problem when she started
school, and that's exactly why you didn't want to hire
me. I'm beginning to understand that now.' She looked
right at him. 'What you wanted,' she said with slow
deliberation, 'what you wanted from the beginning was
not a teacher. You wanted a combination grandmother
and therapist. Well, I'm sorry, but I'm neither. I'm a
teacher, and a good one. I know teaching isn't a
fashionable career these days, and not one that'll ever
make me a lot of money, but it's what I like, it's what
I'm meant to do. I like kids. I enjoy helping them learn
and develop their skills, but what I'm *not* is——'

'I never questioned any of that.'

'Yes, you did! From the beginning. But you didn't
just want a teacher for Anouk; you wanted more. And
it is not reasonable and not fair to expect me to give
therapy to a child with emotional problems. No matter
how much I want to help her, I'm not trained for that.
That's not my role.'

His face hardened. He didn't like to hear those
words: emotional problems. Maybe he considered it a
reflection on himself as a father—the big, successful
man was an incompetent father. Maybe he did not
want to admit that to himself. She felt a swift flash of
pity.

'Anouk is a troubled child,' she said gently. 'I'm
trying, and I'll keep trying, but it may not be enough.'
She paused. 'I would like to know why she doesn't
want to speak English. I would like to know a little
more about her background. It may help me to figure
out what is going on in her mind.'

He closed his eyes briefly and sighed deeply. There were lines of fatigue around his mouth and she felt a sudden softening inside her. He worried about his daughter, and he had hoped that maybe she, the new teacher, could have helped. And she wasn't helping. She wasn't getting anywhere with Anouk. She felt a great sense of failure, which wasn't reasonable, she knew, yet she wished there was something she could do, something to help. She wanted to reach out and touch him, reassure him, but they would only be empty words without any real meaning and she didn't want to do that.

He turned without a word and she watched him go, her heart filled with an odd sense of pain. Or was it something else?

On Sunday afternoon Jason called her on the phone.

'Are you free for dinner tonight?' he asked.

'Dinner?' she echoed in surprise. Was this Jason Grant talking?

'Yes. Food, drink, talk,' he said drily. 'Such as in a restaurant. Semarang isn't known for its elegant dining, but I imagine we can manage to find a decent place.'

Rae was rather thrown off balance by the invitation. She wasn't at all sure she wanted to spend an evening with this man; the idea alone made her nervous.

'Why?' she asked.

'Why what?'

'Why are you asking me out to dinner?'

'I'd like to talk to you,' he said drily.

'You keep saying that, and every time we talk it's a distinctly unpleasant experience.'

'Maybe we should correct that.' There was a touch of humour in his voice. 'I'd appreciate it if you would give me the opportunity to improve the quality of our parent-teacher relationship. How is that?'

She smiled into the phone. 'Very craftily phrased,'

she said lightly, 'and, as such, an offer that's difficult to refuse.'

'At least for a conscientious teacher. So you're saying yes?'

'I don't have much of a choice, do I?'

'I'll try not to make it too much of an ordeal. I'll pick you up at seven.'

Later, as she dressed, taking much too long, Rae couldn't help but wonder why she was so nervous. She looked at herself in the mirror, seeing the brightness in her eyes, wondering about Jason and the deeper feelings that stirred beneath the troubled surface of their relationship.

CHAPTER THREE

'I want to apologise.' Jason looked at her across the small formica table, his eyes holding hers. 'I wasn't fair to you; I wasn't from the beginning.' He smiled ruefully. 'I'm truly sorry.'

Rae frowned. 'I don't understand. Why this sudden change of heart?'

He leaned his arms on the table, the beer bottle clasped between his hands. 'All last night I thought about what you said. It's quite true that I've known something was wrong for a while. Ever since we came to Indonesia, in fact.' He sighed wearily. 'I simply did not want to admit it to myself. Then yesterday. . .' He shrugged. 'I just had to face up to the facts.'

Rae didn't know what to say. She looked around the *warung*, and watched the food being cooked over fires in several enormous oil-drums. There was only a large canvas roof over some forty or fifty small tables arranged in neat rows on the concrete floor.

She glanced back at Jason. Something was wrong with Anouk. It hadn't been so hard to guess, but it was a relief to hear Jason admit it. 'We'll have to find out what it is that's bothering her,' she said. 'I don't think we'll get anywhere without figuring that out first.'

'Maybe it was a mistake to take her away from her grandparents,' he said. 'It was a terrible shock for her when her mother died, but at least she had her grandparents. She settled down in a loving environment and then I took her away to come here. I may be her father, but what I can give her is not enough.' He stared down at his plate, but Rae hadn't missed the bleakness that had flickered briefly in his eyes.

'Somewhere in my mind it became your problem,' he went on. 'You were her teacher, you were supposed to handle her. When things didn't work out it became your fault.' He looked up and gave her a crooked little smile, mocking himself. 'It's warped thinking, and I can't believe I've been so blind and so stupid.' He took her hand and warmth flooded her. His eyes held hers. 'I'm truly sorry for being so unfair to you.'

'It's all right,' she said, her voice unsteady.

'No, it's not. There was no excuse for me to treat you the way I did.' He was still holding her hand, looking into her eyes.

She managed a smile. 'You're forgiven. I survived. It's all in a day's work.' Her voice, mercifully, was light.

'Thank you.' He let go of her hand and leaned back in his chair. The metal scraped across the concrete floor. An awkward silence hung between them. Rae became aware of other noises: the sounds of the traffic out in the street, someone laughing at one of the other tables, the hissing of the fire when fat dripped into it. Scents of the cooking food reached across the open space.

'The food smells great,' she said.

He lifted his bottle of beer and drank from it. 'The décor, however, leaves much to be desired.'

She laughed. 'It's hard when there are no walls to work with. But I like it. Real Java ambience.'

Western sophistication was hard to find in Semarang restaurants, where basic plastic was the standard. When Jason had asked her for her choice of restaurant, she'd asked to come here, to a *warung*, and eat Indonesian style, which had both surprised and pleased him. 'Well, if you want good food, that's the place to go,' he'd said. 'As long as you don't mind formica tables and folding chairs.'

Rae drank her beer and watched the waiter come

across the room balancing an overloaded tray of bar-
becued delicacies. They'd ordered squid, shrimp and a
pork dish.

'Have you lived overseas before?' she asked. 'Don't
you find it interesting to eat in places like this?'

'Sometimes. I've done a lot of travelling in Africa,
but the food is better in the East. And I lived in Bolivia
for a while. *Churasco* is popular there, charcoal-roasted
meat. Not your ordinary steak, mind you, but slabs
well over a pound.'

'Do you like living overseas, or do you do it because
you have to?'

'I don't do much because I have to. I do like living
overseas. I'm not crazy about the short-term contracts;
there's never a chance to really learn anything about a
place.' He took a swig of his beer. 'After a few years I
do get tired and want to get back home for a while, to
a place where at least you can rely on a steady supply
of electricity and water and a telephone system that
works. But then, after a while. . .' he smiled '. . .after
a while I want out again. Gypsy blood, I guess. Once
you have the itch, it stays in your system.'

The food was placed in front of them and Rae ate
with appetite, asking him questions about his travels
and his work as a business management consultant.
The tension between them had eased and it was
possible now to speak to him without the guardedness
she had experienced before. He was an interesting
man, but she had known that already, yet now she
could allow herself to ask him questions, to get beyond
the initial suspicion. His admission had surprised her;
it showed him to be a man who wanted to be honest
with himself and others.

He had been honest with her. She felt a sense of
warmth at the thought, a thrill of some deeper feeling.
She looked at him across the table and he caught her
gaze and smiled.

'It's good, isn't it?'

'Yes. Thank you for asking me out. I'm enjoying this. I was getting really tired of fast food or frozen dinners. In the States, I mean. I never seemed to have time to cook myself something fresh and unadulterated. Here there's time for eating and talking with friends. People do things together, spend time together.'

He eyed her speculatively. 'Is that why you came back here?'

She nodded. 'I never knew how rushed my life really was, had always been until I came here. I, we. . .' She swallowed. 'My husband and I loved it here. Then when we went back to the States I told myself I wouldn't get caught up in the mad dashing around, but I had no choice. It's the way life is at home, at least in New York. I wanted to go to college, but I had to work to support myself. I was doing everything, racing around all over the place, with never a moment's time to breathe.'

She'd felt lost and lonely after Matt had died and all the work and studying had at least kept her mind occupied, but it had also prevented her from making friends and meeting men. There had never been any time. The few men who had shown interest in her she had not encouraged. It was too soon. She had felt nothing and nobody appealed to her. At odd moments she had worried about it. What if she was going to be single for the rest of her life? What if she never found another man to love? But she'd pushed the thoughts away and concentrated on her work. At night she'd fallen into bed, too exhausted to think or worry.

She speared a shrimp and ate it. 'I promised myself that as soon as I had my degree I would get out of New York and go somewhere more relaxed.'

'With your ESL degree you can go anywhere.'

She nodded. 'I know. It's an exciting idea to think

that I can find work the world over. Like having wings.'
She grinned. 'As a kid I always wanted wings. It
seemed to me the ultimate in freedom.' She looked
down at her plate and finished the last of her rice. 'I
didn't know I'd come back to Semarang, but I'm glad.
I still have friends here, and I knew the place, so it was
easier getting settled in.' She grimaced. 'Of course,
everybody thought I was crazy. My family wanted me
to get a job in some good school in New York. I
couldn't wait to get out.'

'Most people wouldn't like it here.'

'My friend Kate would be back on the next flight.'
She laughed. 'Actually, she'd probably never get on a
flight to come over in the first place.'

She saw Kate in her mind's eye, with her big, hungry
grey eyes, her sleek black hair shaped in a short boyish
style, her oversized dangling earrings. Kate, always
running in five different directions looking for the
perfect man.

'You're crazy to go back over there,' Kate had said,
sitting cross-legged on Rae's floor, eating anchovy
pizza. 'Stay here where at least you can find another
man, settle down, have a life.' Tact wasn't Kate's
strong point.

'I'm not looking for a man,' Rae said, which was
true enough. 'And even if I were, this doesn't seem to
be a promising place, if you believe what everybody
says. The good ones are married or buried or hiding in
Alaska. I believe those were your words?'

Kate shrugged. 'What are you going to find on Java?
Short skinny men who don't speak English and eat
garlic and want to marry you for your money.'

Rae almost choked on her pizza. 'All seventy-six
dollars. God, you're a bigot, Kate.'

'I'm a realist and I hate garlic.' She took a big
swallow of red wine.

'Java is a great place. And there are some very

handsome men with lots of money, to set the record
straight.'

Kate frowned. 'Oil, isn't it?'

'Yes, and rubber and tea and a few other things.'

'Well, maybe there's hope for you yet. If it looks
good, let me know and I'll come over.'

'I think you should stay here.' Rae smiled sweetly.
'New York deserves you.'

Rae glanced at Jason. Kate would probably think
Jason was the perfect man, or at least close to it. She'd
found a lot of perfect men, who later turned out to be
flawed in major or minor ways. They didn't have
enough money, they snored in their sleep, they were
married, they lived with their mothers. Jason, no
doubt, had his flaws, some of which Rae had already
discovered. She'd probably discover a few more.

Right now he didn't look too flawed. He was being
positively interesting company. He was handsome. She
liked looking at his hands, his hair, his eyes. She liked
the feeling of his big hand holding hers. She wondered
what it would be like to be kissed by him, to be made
love to by him. She bit her lip hard and looked away.
Jason Grant was doing terrible things to her mind.

A flaw she might discover in herself was the lack of
resistance to his male appeal, the confident, easy way
he moved his tall body, the thick black hair, the blue,
blue eyes that were looking at her right now.

'What are you thinking about?' he asked. 'You were
staring.'

'Flaws,' she said, amazed at her prompt response.

He raised a thick eyebrow. 'Flaws? Well, I'm sure
you've discovered I have some.'

'I was thinking of my own.'

He smiled a true blue delighted smile. 'Tell me about
your flaws.'

She laughed. 'Some are better left hidden but, well,
let me see.' She frowned. 'I'm pig-headed, they all tell

me, and I have a serious lack of good sense, and I'm a glutton for good chocolate.'

'And you agree with those observations?'

She grinned. 'Oh, absolutely.'

'What about your good points?'

'They're very boring.'

His eyes sparked with humour. 'Boring is not a term I'd apply to you. I'm already discovering that.'

'Thank you,' she said lightly. She pushed her plate away and wiped her mouth on a small napkin. 'That was delicious.'

They drove home through the dark, quiet streets, talking easily, and Rae couldn't help feeling a warm sense of elation—a lightness of spirit that she hadn't felt for a long, long time.

As they drove up through the gates, Nicky came to the door, wearing a long, loose dress in several exuberant shades of violet and pink. She looked rather exotic as she stood there, the breeze gently stirring the soft material around her legs.

'Do you want to come in for a drink?' she asked. 'Kevin is here, and he brought us some wine from the Aussie commissary in Jakarta. You don't want to miss that.'

They followed her out to the veranda and sampled the Australian wine, listening to Kevin, dressed in ragged shorts and disreputable sneakers, extolling the virtues of his native brew. It looked as if his face hadn't seen a razor for two or three days.

'I thought you were more of a beer man,' Rae said, and he gave her a wounded look. 'You never did appreciate the more sophisticated side of me. You foreigners think all we do is drink beer and herd sheep.'

Rae reached out and touched his hand. 'It's a burden, I'm sure,' she said, grinning. 'Just keep building your bridges and bringing us your wine and we may change our minds.'

'We know you sail boats pretty good,' Nicky said soothingly.

Kevin tugged at Rae's hand and leaned closer. 'I'll convince you yet,' he said darkly, 'that some of us have soft cores and appreciate the finer things in life.'

'First,' Rae said, 'you shave.'

Nicky laughed and promptly choked on her wine.

Jason came to his feet. 'I must be going.' Rae watched him, seeing some unfathomable look in his eyes. She got up too, wondering why he was leaving so early, if the conversation was boring him.

'Did we bore you?' she asked, as she let him out of the door and he gave her a crooked smile. 'No, not in the least.' His gaze locked with hers for a long moment and she stood very still, her heart suddenly taking off in some fast, nervous rhythm.

'Thank you for dinner,' she said brightly, trying to cover up her unease. 'I enjoyed it.'

'So did I.' Then he leaned forward and kissed her mouth, very quickly, turned and got into the car.

He waved as he drove off and she stood in the door, unmoving, her emotions in turmoil.

Don't be a fool, she said to herself. It was nothing. It wasn't even a real kiss. Nothing more meaningful than a quick handshake. A polite thanks-for-the-nice-evening-goodnight sort of kiss.

She went back to the veranda and had another glass of wine. Maybe it would help her sleep.

The Germans among the expatriates had outdone themselves. Putting on an Oktoberfest in the tropics was no mean feat, but they had certainly given it their all. Beer-hall music assaulted Rae's ears as she arrived at the Kelly house.

'I wonder if the Indonesian neighbours appreciate this sort of music,' Nicky said as they climbed out of the car.

Rae thought of the gentle, sentimental music and the swaying, undulating bodies of the dancing girls of the entertainment programme she'd watched a few times on television. 'Somehow, I doubt it,' she said.

David locked the car and pocketed the key. 'I think they were all invited to the party. They are every year, but they never come.'

The yard had been transformed into a facsimile of a German beer-hall with long tables and benches set out under cover of large canvas canopies to protect them from the inevitable rain. Candles and coloured lights burned cheerfully in the dark.

They were greeted by Kurt Reinecker, wearing lederhosen and looking utterly ridiculous. He handed them each a shot glass half-full of schnapps, the drinking of which was the prerequisite for joining the party. Only the most serious of reasons was acceptable as an excuse. Bravely, Rae downed the fiery liquid, grimacing as it went down her throat.

'You should be deported for forcing us to drink this,' she said, handing back the shot glass. He grinned and hung a gigantic Bavarian bread pretzel on a ribbon around her neck. No one without a pretzel was allowed on the premises, and it was meant to be nibbled on during the festivities.

'This is a really classy affair, let me tell you,' Nicky said, taking a bite from her pretzel. 'I love it.'

'If you've got any inhibitions,' David said to Rae, 'this is the place to lose them, especially after two or three in the morning.'

The three advanced into the yard, the delicious aroma of a roasting suckling pig wafting through the air. There was German beer and German food of every variety that the women had spent days cooking and baking. Vast quantities of sausages had been ordered from Germany.

'Let's drink and be merry,' David suggested.

'Let's eat,' Nicky said soberly. 'I'm starved. I want some of that bread before it's gone. It's the absolute best bread in the world.'

Rae surveyed the crowd, wondering if Jason was among it, but she didn't see him. She hadn't seen him during the past week, except for a few minutes each morning as he'd dropped Anouk off at school. Maybe this was not his kind of party, although even the stuffiest of the British seemed to be enjoying themselves. She felt acute disappointment, which irritated her. Then, when he did arrive, not much later, her heart went berserk as she saw him approach. She closed her eyes for a moment. *What is the matter with me?* she asked herself. *This is not normal.*

'Have you eaten yet?' he asked.

She shook her head. 'No. I was waiting for the pig. A piece of it, anyway.'

'They're slicing it now.' He glanced around the table. 'Quite a spread they're putting on.'

'Nicky told me they do it every year. I missed it when I was here before.'

They ate, they talked. People were dancing, laughing, singing bawdy German drinking songs and having a wonderful time.

Rae danced until she felt silly with exhaustion—with Joost, Hillie's husband, with David and Kurt and Kevin, who was a little unsteady on his legs. He held her a little too closely. He stepped on her toes. He said she was the most beautiful woman at the party, and if he ever made the mistake of marrying again, she'd be the lucky one.

Jason rescued her.

'The man is drunk,' he said with ill-concealed disgust as he swung her away.

Jason certainly was not. He was very steady indeed.

'Not really,' Rae said. 'He's naturally clumsy.'

'You seem to know him well.'

'He was here when I lived here before. We were good friends.'

He did not reply, moving her easily around the other dancers.

'You don't like him,' she stated. He hadn't actually said it, but it wasn't hard to guess.

He looked down at her, his mouth tilted. 'What I've seen of him doesn't impress me greatly.'

'Well, you don't know him.' She didn't know why she felt she should defend Kevin. He certainly wasn't the most perfect of human beings, but then who was?

He gave her a narrow-eyed look. 'No, I suppose I don't.'

'I know he comes across as being a little rough around the edges, and he lives a little loose and easy, but he has a very soft heart.' She suspected Kevin was rather insecure, which he covered up with bravado, but she didn't say it.

'A soft heart?' He gave her a sceptical look. 'That's hard to see, indeed, but please let's not discuss Kevin North.'

Somebody had changed the music into something dreadfully schmaltzy, which caused a few groans from the dancers. Jason didn't ask if she wanted to sit down, but merely drew her closer and moved to the slow rhythm of the music. A sentimental voice sang a maudlin German song and several of the Germans were wailing right along.

'Only the Dutch can do worse,' Jason said, rolling his eyes, and Rae laughed.

It felt good to be in his arms. Too good. She leaned her head against his shoulder. She was exhausted, and the mere two glasses of wine had gone straight to her head. 'I wish they wouldn't play everything so loud.'

'I turned it down a couple of times already. They turn it right back up.'

They were talking, yet she felt, under the surface,

the stirring of something else. It was impossible not to
be aware of their bodies touching—the weight of his
hand on her back, her breasts brushing against his
chest, thighs touching thighs. She was aware of the
warmth of him against her and the clean scent of his
skin. Her every nerve tingled with sensation. It was
frightening to think how easily her body reacted to his
closeness.

'I'd better sit down,' she said when the music ended,
hoping her voice was as light as she intended. 'My feet
are giving out.'

The party got a little out of hand after that, with the
playing of silly games, more singing and dancing. A
rock-lifting contest was in full swing. They watched as
one man after another tried to lift the rock, an enormous boulder impervious to the strain of many backs.
There was loud cheering as finally Kevin, with his
bulky frame, managed to tilt it sideways, which was as
far as he could manage it. With a groan he released the
rock, which rolled back in its original position, nearly
squashing his foot.

'You look like you've about had it,' Jason said. 'If
you want to leave, I'll take you home.'

Rae glanced over at Nicky and David. They seemed
to be having a good time, talking and laughing as they
watched some strange-looking finger-pulling game.

'If you don't mind,' she said, getting up from the
bench.

'No,' he said, smiling, 'I don't mind.'

It was a relief to get away from the noise. It was
after midnight and the dark streets were deserted. The
watchman was asleep on his mat in front of the gate
and jumped up hastily when they approached and
opened the gate.

Rae hesitated as she got out of the car.

'Would you like some coffee?' she asked. 'To recu-
perate from all the fun and games?'

'I'd like that, thank you.' He sounded so formal, it made her smile.

'You don't have to be polite, you know. We could just sit on the veranda and soak in the quiet.'

His mouth quirked. 'Who needs coffee?'

All the games we play, she thought, as they moved to the big veranda.

It was very quiet, very peaceful, with only the crickets making their nightly mating chirpings. In the kampong everything was silent; people had gone to bed long ago. In the distance lay the Java Sea, dark and silent under a pale half-moon.

Rae leaned against the railing, feeling oddly restless. Jason stood beside her, reaching out to touch her hair. She could hear her heart hammering.

'It's such a beautiful night,' he said quietly.

'Yes.' Her mouth went dry. She didn't dare look at him, afraid he would see her emotions in her face.

'I enjoyed dancing with you,' he said softly.

She nodded, not trusting her voice.

'Would you like to dance to some other kind of music?' he asked. 'I'm sure Nicky and David must have something better than drinking songs.'

'We could have a look,' she heard herself say. 'The tape deck is in the living-room.'

They sat on their haunches in front of the cabinet that held the tapes, close, very close, with arms touching—gentle, seemingly accidental touches. And she sat in breathless silence as she blindly searched through the titles, seeing nothing, hearing nothing, just trem-blingly aware of the warmth of his body radiating on her skin, his face close to hers. She watched his hand as it moved along the row of tapes, seeing the long, strong fingers, thinking how beautiful his hand was, longing to be touched.

'How about this one?' He lifted the tape out of its slot with deft fingers. His voice was soft, his eyes quiet as he smiled at her, and she knew that he was quite aware of the tension hovering between them.

She nodded. 'That's fine.' Her voice sounded strange, and she came slowly to her feet as Jason put the tape on.

Moments later she was in his arms, their bodies moving to something gentle and sensuous. She felt light and alive, her every nerve aware of his body so close to hers, the warmth of him, the male scent of him. The heady excitement filled her with a deep, treacherous longing. It was wonderful, it was frightening. She wanted to stay. She wanted to run to the safety of her room and lock the door to him, to the aching need in her body.

The music came to an end, but he did not release her. His arms tightened around her and she felt the heat of his body, the need reflecting her own.

'I like holding you.'

She felt her body begin to tremble. She hoped he didn't feel it. There was a danger in closeness, in opening herself up to all the feelings of need and longing. A danger full of risks of hurt and disappointment and loss. Yet a danger so exciting, so hopeful and glorious, she could not resist the temptation.

The room faded away, and there was only the light of his eyes, a blue fire so intense that she felt the heat of it in her blood.

He bent his head and lowered his mouth to hers.

Warmth, softness, a spiralling of heat. Behind her closed eyelids there were stars, falling stars, and colour, so much beautiful colour. No thoughts. A rush of pure sensation: his mouth, so full of rich pleasure as he touched her lips, his tongue finding hers in a dance of pure delight. A searching—giving and asking. Her blood singing and a headiness so full of starry longing that she no longer felt her feet on the floor. Drifting, floating, with his arms around her and nothing, nothing was more delicious, nothing freer and wilder than his kiss.

He released her slowly and for an endless moment they just looked at each other. She felt as if she'd come back from some faraway place, some other sphere of consciousness, and she didn't want to come back, be here in the shadowed room with the dark shapes of furniture and the overhead fan stirring the heavy air.

But the stars were gone now and her blood had stilled its mad rushing. Jason reached out and touched her cheek, a soft, gentle caress. Then he took a step back, moving towards the door.

'Goodnight, Rae.'

She lay in bed, still trembling, her face pressed into the pillow.

'You're a grown, mature woman,' she said to herself. 'Don't make up any excuses for what you are feeling. You know what it is.'

Lust, that was what Kate would have called it. Lust is good, lust is healthy, she would have said. You're finally coming back to life. Hallelujah.

Rae turned over on her back and stared at the ceiling. It was an ugly word. She didn't like it. It wasn't what she was feeling.

What, then? Passion? Desire?

She didn't like those words, either. Maybe there were no words for what she was feeling. She wanted to make love. She wanted Jason to touch her and kiss her. She wanted her body to come alive and feel the glorious, heady delights of loving.

She sat up abruptly and turned on the bedside lamp. On the dresser was Matt's photo, his face smiling at her across the room. Tears rushed into her eyes, blurring her vision.

'Oh, damn,' she muttered. 'Oh, damn.' She got out of bed and picked up the photo, wiping her eyes.

'I'm sorry,' she whispered, 'but you're not there any more. I need someone to love. I can't help it.'

The familiar face kept smiling at her. There was no reproof, no censure in the brown eyes.

'All right, then,' she whispered.

She opened a drawer and carefully put the picture away.

After school on Tuesday, she was shopping at Gelael supermarket and almost collided with Hillie Moerman, who looked spring-fresh in a yellow sun-dress. Rae felt hot and sticky, and she wiped a damp curl behind her ear as she said hello to Hillie.

'Rae! Hello!' Hillie pushed her shopping trolley out of the way. 'I want to tell you,' she said, 'I'm impressed. Sander and Miranda are learning English so quickly. Suddenly they are doing it so much better.'

Rae smiled, warmth flooding her. It was good to hear an appreciative word. It seemed as though her day was filled with thoughts of Anouk and how to draw her out. 'Oh, thank you, but I can't take all the credit. Just being with the other English-speaking children in school is probably the biggest help.' She sighed. 'I'm not having much success with Anouk Grant, I'm afraid.'

Hillie shook her head and ran her fingers through the short, wavy hair. 'Poor Anouk.' She gave Rae a searching look. 'The children say she's sitting alone now, and she's not allowed to work with the others.'

Rae felt a sudden urge to defend herself. It made her sound like an ogre of a teacher to separate Anouk from the rest of the students instead of giving her tender loving care. Well, TLC hadn't worked.

'She doesn't want to participate in the work,' she said, hoping her voice didn't sound too defensive.

'She's a very stubborn little thing.' Hillie stepped aside to let a woman pass. 'You know, she told me before school started that she didn't want to go to that "stupid" school in a house. She wanted to go to a real school, like the one she would have gone to in Holland. It had red doors and a big playground and a real gym-room with all sorts of wonderful. . .er, bars, rings. . .*stuff*,' she finished with a frustrated grin.

'Equipment,' Rae supplied.

Hillie sighed. 'I don't know why I can't remember that word. Anyway,' she said with a grin, 'Anouk wants red doors and gym equipment.'

'We've got blue doors,' Rae said.

Hillie's eyes were laughing. 'But that's not red. When Anouk gets something into her head, it's hard to get it out. She and my Miranda play several times a week and I know how stubborn she is. She's with us now.' She blew at her fringe, then impatiently wiped it aside. 'Listen, are you busy now? Would you like to come to my house to drink tea?'

Rae smiled at her. 'I'd like that.' Hillie knew Anouk. Maybe there was something she could learn from Hillie.

The house was large and a bit shabby, but Hillie had made something warm and homey out of it with batik art on the walls and lots of cushions and cosy lamps. It was a home alive with children and noise and laughter. They sat on the veranda with their tea and watched all five of them play with a brown puppy with floppy ears.

Hillie told her that the family had arrived in Semarang only three weeks before Jason and Anouk. Miranda and Anouk were the same age and had struck up an instant friendship. 'She spends a lot of time here. I think she's lonely and she misses her grandparents. They lived with them after her mother died.'

'I know. Jason told me.' She hesitated. 'Do you know how his wife died?'

'A car accident. A truck-driver with too much of everything in his system ran into her. She'd just dropped Anouk off at her cousin's house, which was a blessing, if you can talk of blessings.' She shuddered. 'Jason doesn't talk about it.'

In the silence Rae heard the excited voices of the children. She watched Anouk play, listened to her laugh. The girl's wiry body was constantly in motion and she seemed eager to order everybody around.

'Anouk likes it here because of the family atmosphere,' she said to Hillie. 'Because you're Dutch, because it feels like home to her.'

Hillie nodded. 'I know Jason tries, but it's just him, and he's a man. I know that sounds chauvinistic, but it's difficult to fill the place of a mother. I know he's home at three or four every afternoon. He works at home a lot and he starts at the godless hour of six or seven.' She waved at a fly buzzing around her head. 'He gives her plenty of time and attention; it isn't that. He takes her swimming at the pool a couple of times a week. On weekends all of us sometimes go to Jepara beach, although I dread going with my four. It's a long drive and there's no shade on the beach, but they do love it.' She paused and stirred her tea, then slowly looked back at Rae. There was hesitation in her eyes.

'Jason is terribly lonely, too,' she said quietly. 'I know he seems quite self-contained and under control, but you know how it is with men; they don't show their emotions easily.'

'I know.' Rae stared at her coral-polished toenails, thinking of Matt. 'Or it comes out in other ways.' She glanced back at Hillie, aware that the other woman was trying to tell her something, but wasn't sure how to go about it.

'Yes.' Hillie hesitated again. 'He was angry and upset with you those first few weeks.'

Rae grimaced. 'He expected me to solve all Anouk's problems. I am the teacher, I should know how to handle her.'

'But that wasn't the only reason; you know that.'

Rae slowly shook her head. 'No, I. . .I don't know what you mean.'

Hillie put her cup down on the table. 'He was very attracted to you from the beginning, and he didn't want that. I think it frightened him. It took him by surprise and it made him angry. At himself, at you.'

Rae felt a breathless lightness invade her. 'Did he tell you that?'

Hillie laughed. 'No. I'm only guessing.' She placed her hand on her heart. 'But my intuition is very good.'

'Do you know him well?'

'He and Anouk spend a lot of time here. After half a year I think I know him a little.'

Rae didn't know what to say. This information needed time to digest, but she felt a joy warming her body, her heart. She felt a restless excitement, a sense of aliveness. She was aware of the warm air touching her skin, the breeze stirring the palm fronds.

'I don't know you well,' Hillie said, 'but I like you, and I don't think you would play games with him and hurt him on purpose. That's why I wanted to tell you.' Her wide mouth tilted in a knowing half smile. 'I saw you both at the Oktoberfest. You're not immune to him, are you?'

Rae shook her head and sighed. 'No.' She felt exposed. Her feelings were too new and confusing to share, even with Hillie who cared and who seemed to understand.

A wail from the garden broke the awkward silence. One of the twins had fallen and scraped a knee. Kisses were dispensed, along with some first-aid cream and a biscuit.

A car drove up the driveway and a moment later Jason, dressed casually in blue denim shorts and a white T-shirt, appeared around the corner of the house. Muscular brown legs leaped easily up the veranda steps. 'Hello, ladies,' he said, smiling at them both. His gaze held Rae's a moment longer, and she felt her stomach muscles tighten and her heart suddenly thundered against her ribs. For one endless moment it was Saturday night again and his mouth was on hers, her body trembling in his arms.

'Sit down,' Hillie ordered, 'and I'll pour you some tea. You look tired.'

'Tired but victorious,' he said with a grin. 'I finally convinced a few key people of the folly of their plan. They've decided to do it my way.'

'Now it had better work,' Hillie said drily, 'whatever it is.'

'Oh, it will.' He sounded supremely confident. He stretched out in the chair and put his hands behind his head and gazed contentedly up into the palms above. Hillie poured all three of them a cup of tea from the big pot.

Rae began to breathe a little more easily. She wondered if her thoughts had been visible on her face, if Jason guessed what had gone through her mind. Maybe it had gone through his mind as well.

Jason glanced over at Rae. 'So, how did my daughter do today?'

'Same as last week. No change.'

He frowned. 'I've decided that I'm going to speak English to her at home. We simply have to break down that stubbornness.'

'I don't think that's a good idea,' Hillie offered. 'It shouldn't be a power struggle.' She waved her hand apologetically. 'Not that it is any of my business.'

'I just want to try it.'

A horde of kids came tumbling up on to the veranda, and a flood of excited Dutch filled the air. Anouk came up to her father and gave him a hug. He kissed her on the cheek, then turned to the other children and said something which made them all jump up and down and cheer.

'He promised to take them all to the pool at the Patra Jasa Hotel,' Hillie said to Rae. 'He told them to get their things while he drinks his tea.'

The children raced indoors to put on their swimsuits and get their towels. Hillie grimaced. 'Mob control in order here.' She got up and followed them in.

Jason grinned at Rae. 'You want to come along for a swim? There are only five of them. Piece of cake.'

She laughed. 'You can handle it.'

His eyes smiled into hers. 'I'd like it if you'd come.'

As she looked into his eyes, all she could think of was his mouth on hers, his arms holding her against him.

'A swim sounds good,' she said.

CHAPTER FOUR

IT HAD probably been a mistake to go for a swim, Rae thought, as she slipped out of her shorts and top. She felt suddenly awfully naked, despite her swimsuit. Swimsuits weren't designed to hide anything, she was quite aware of that, but with Jason right there she couldn't help but feel self-conscious. She was uneasily aware of her small breasts and the birthmark on her left thigh.

Jason was wearing black trunks, and his strong, muscular body was tanned all over. She eyed him surreptitiously, taking inventory, as he helped Hillie's twins with their swimming-wings. Wide shoulders, narrow hips, flat stomach—a perfect male physique. Dark hair formed a light mat on his chest and he looked fit and healthily male. She looked at the warm gleam of his dark skin and wanted to touch him, kiss him. There was a restless fluttering inside her, a weakness in her stomach. She bit her lip to quell the shakiness and looked away. She folded her clothes and put them down next to her towel on the lounger.

She helped Miranda tie the strings of her swimsuit and told everybody to put their flipflops under the loungers so no one would trip over them. When she looked again, Jason was fixing Anouk's hair into a ponytail while the others stood waiting for her impatiently. When Anouk joined them they all held hands and stood poised at the pool's edge. The four-year-old twins with their orange safety-wings looked like clumsy little birds teetering at the edge of the nest.

'*Een, twee, drie!*' they yelled at the tops of their voices. At the count of three they all jumped in and raced across the width of the pool. Sander, who was eight and very strong, came in first, with Anouk close behind. She climbed out and stood dripping, a determined look on her face. In her blue-striped swimsuit she looked even thinner than in her clothes.

'Don't you feed her?' Rae asked Jason after the children took off on another race. He groaned.

'She lives on air. All she wants is junk food—biscuits and cake—but I won't let her have much. She had a medical before we left and the doctor said she's perfectly healthy. If she's hungry, she'll eat, he said.' Jason grimaced. 'I hope she gets hungry one of these days, just so I don't have to eat alone.' His eyes slipped over Rae in quick appraisal and she hugged her arms in front of her chest. She bit her lip, noticing a gleam of humour in his eyes, which annoyed her no end.

'What are you laughing at?' she snapped.

His eyebrows rose in innocent question. 'Nothing. I'm not laughing.'

'Don't look at me like that!'

'Like what?'

'You know like what.' She sighed. 'Sorry, I'm being stupid.'

'It's hard not to look at you, when you're standing right there in front of me.' He laughed. 'Relax. I'll keep my eyes under control.'

She looked at him dubiously and his mouth tilted in a smile. 'What I'm really interested in I saw long ago.'

'And what is that?'

'Eyes.' His gaze held hers and she felt her body begin to glow. He reached out and touched a finger to her lips. 'And mouths,' he added softly. His hand dropped by his side. 'And you have beautiful, expressive eyes and a very kissable mouth.'

She wanted to give some smart answer, something to the effect that he had a great line, but she wasn't falling

for it, but she sensed that his words were quite sincere
and she was silent.

The children were shouting for him to come in. 'I'll
go do my duty,' he said, and took a clean dive into the
water. When he came up again he shook the water out
of his hair and gestured at her to come in, too. She was
still standing at the edge of the pool, Jason's words
echoing in her head.

She dived in, and for the next twenty minutes they
all played games and held races. She enjoyed watching
Jason rough-house with the children; it was a side of
him she hadn't seen before. He carried them on his
shoulders, dumping them in head first, or giving them
a flying leap. They shrieked with excitement. Anouk
was as wild as the boys, but ignored Rae completely in
any of the games they played.

Leaving the children to their own devices, they
climbed out and sat on the loungers in the late-
afternoon sun. Jason ordered drinks from the hotel
bar, and Rae sipped her gin and tonic slowly as she
watched the children play.

'Are you coming to Sarangan?' he asked.

She nodded. 'Nicky convinced me that after two
months I most definitely need a break, so I guess I'll
defy the cliffs and hairpin turns. They say Sarangan is
beautiful and cool and quiet. Have you been there
before?'

'No, but I wouldn't mind a little change of scenery
at all. I'll have to go to Jakarta for a couple of days this
week, and next week I'll be totally tied up with some
jokers from Washington. I'll be happy to get a little
cooling-off time. Needless to say, I have little choice
anyway, with Anouk bugging me to go.' He grinned.
'She heard stories about boats and horseback rides and
other delights.

'There's a wooded island in the middle of the lake,
I'm told. The Moerman kids are planning to play Dr

Livingstone.' She smiled up at the sky, squinting against the light. 'They're a nice family.'

'Yes, they are.' The tone of his voice made her look back at him. He met her eyes, smiling ruefully.

'We didn't have much luck, did we?'

She swallowed at the lump in her throat. 'No.' All the old pain was back, and she looked away, the colours blurring in front of her eyes. She thought of Josie's baby, of the family she would never have with Matt.

'Maybe we'll get another chance.'

She didn't answer. She didn't trust herself to speak. Then she felt his hand, warm on hers, clasping it in the solid strength of his.

'Don't you want to?'

She could feel her heart racing, a sudden breathless feeling in her chest. Everything seemed to have gone silent around them. No longer did she hear the children's excited voices, nor the birds' twitter in the bushes. She looked down at their hands, locked together on the edge of her chair.

'Yes, I do,' she said.

The days that followed were vague and hazy, as if she weren't consciously living them. Her body went through the motions, but her mind was somewhere else.

There were so many doubts—fear and shivering hope. So many thoughts whirling through her head as she sat by herself reading, not reading, lying in bed wide-eyed and awake with his face in her mind, his words in her ears.

The fear. Will it be all right? Will it just be a disappointment? Maybe he is not what I think he is. Maybe it's better not to hope. . .

But the hope was there, filling the emptiness, the

loneliness of the last two years. Hope for love and happiness, for feeling alive with joy.

There was Kate's voice, cold and cynical after another broken love-affair. Don't believe in fairy-tales, Rae. There's no happy ending, ever, you know that. Somehow they always desert you, betray you, dump you, one way or another.

Like by dying, Rae had thought silently. Maybe, she had said carefully, you shouldn't look for the perfect man, Kate. You set yourself up for disappointment. Nobody is perfect, but you don't have to be perfect to be lovable.

At night she sat up in bed, hoping, dreaming, her book unread on her lap, absently watching some tiny pink lizard scoot across the wall.

She didn't see Jason for the rest of the week. Anouk was staying with the Moerman family while Jason was in Jakarta. On Friday afternoon Rae was in the kitchen with Nicky, getting ready for a dinner party, when the phone rang.

'It's Jason, for you,' Nicky said, handing the receiver over.

'Jason? So you're back from the big city.'

'I just walked in the door. How are you?'

'Fine. Up to my elbows in whipped cream.'

He laughed. 'Sounds delicious. Can I see you tonight?'

Tonight. Seven people for dinner. Disappointment settled heavy in her stomach. 'We have a dinner party here. I can't leave.' Her mind searched for a possibility. It wasn't such a big affair that she could sneak off unnoticed.

'Go,' Nicky said, grinning maliciously. 'We don't need you.'

'Nicky says I can go. She says they don't need me.'

'She's such a generous person, a real friend. Tell her I said thank you.'

Rae turned to Nicky, who was slicing mangoes, her hands dripping with the orange juice. 'Jason says you're a real friend and to tell you thank you.'

'Anything for love,' Nicky said.

'What was that she said?' Jason asked.

'She said you're welcome.'

'Liar,' Nicky muttered under her breath.

'How about eight at my place for a drink?' he asked. 'I have to stay around the house; I'm expecting a phone call from New York.'

'I'll be there.'

'Will I be depriving you of dinner?'

'Yes, but I'll live. If Ibu is in a good mood she'll let me have something earlier.' Dinner probably wouldn't be served until eight-thirty or so.

'Tell Ibu *terima kasih*, too.'

She laughed. 'I will. I'll see you around eight.'

They finished making the dessert just before five when Ibu came back into the kitchen to claim her territory and prepare the rest of the food.

'She's quite put out when I do anything at all,' Nicky said, 'but I enjoy cooking. She thinks I don't trust her cooking or something. She keeps telling me to show her what I want and then she'll do it, and she probably would, too. She can't read or write, but she sure has a memory.'

Rae took a long, leisurely bath, washed her hair and polished the nails of her fingers and toes. Then, wrapped in her robe, she went to the kitchen in search of some dinner and to cut three generous helpings of the mango torte to take with her to Jason's later. Ibu looked at the torte suspiciously and Rae laughed.

'We're just crazy, Ibu,' she said, guessing that the old woman didn't think much of the mistress of the house pottering in the kitchen when she paid a cook to do the job.

It was still early, so after she'd dressed in a soft blue dress she joined the party on the veranda where they were having drinks and appetisers. At eight she made her apologies and left. Kevin, who had dropped by and promptly been invited to stay, gave her a lecherous wink. Of course everybody knew where she was going.

She walked slowly up the road, around the corner and up to Jason's house, carefully carrying the plate. A small dog yelped at her heels and kept her company till she reached the gate.

'I brought us some dessert,' she said to Jason, handing him the plate. 'Is Anouk still up?'

He shook his head. 'She went to bed about half an hour ago.'

There was something in his voice that made her look at him more closely.

'Is something wrong?'

'She had a terrible tantrum. I'm speaking English to her now and it's not working.' He moved towards the kitchen with the plate and she followed him. He put two pieces of the torte on smaller plates and found some forks in a drawer.

Rae covered the third piece and put it in the refrigerator. She felt a hollow ache in her stomach, which had nothing to do with hunger. 'What does she say when you talk to her?'

'She says I don't love her any more. That she wants to go back to Holland and live with her grandparents and go to school there.'

'Oh, Jason.' Rae's heart contracted with pity. 'I'm so sorry. Why don't you stop?'

'I will. She cried herself to sleep tonight, and also earlier in the week before I went to Jakarta. I can't do this to her.' He grimaced. 'I can't do it to myself.'

'Did Hillie say anything?'

'She was fine over there.' He walked out to the veranda and they sat down. Rae looked at his face, seeing the worry in his eyes. She wished she could go up to him and put her arms around him and wipe away the sadness from his face, but she stayed in the chair, feeling helpless.

She'd made no progress herself. Anouk showed no signs of giving up and joining the others. She was sitting quietly by herself, doing all her paperwork neatly and remaining obstinately silent. Talking to her had no effect whatsoever.

They ate the mango torte. 'This is delicious,' he said, smiling. 'I'm a sucker for whipped cream—the real thing, that is, not that gassed-up stuff from a can.' He put the plate down on the table. 'My wife used to like to make cakes; not the American kind with frosting, but with fruit toppings and whipped cream.'

Rae couldn't think of a thing to say apart from, oh, how nice, or, how delicious, or something else equally inane. He gave a crooked smile when she didn't answer.

'It's not easy talking about my wife.'

She looked into her eyes. 'I know.'

'I don't know what to say, or if I should say anything at all.'

'I don't know, either.'

A slow smile played around his lips. She was glad he could see a little humour in the situation.

'What was her name?' she asked.

'Sandra.'

She nodded. 'Why don't we play it by ear? You talk about her whenever it's comfortable.'

'It won't bother you?'

'I don't know. Would it bother you if I talked about my husband?'

'I don't know.'

Their eyes locked in mutual understanding and she

felt an odd quivering deep inside her. There was the fragile beginning of something special, a careful reaching out. Whatever happened between them could not erase the past, the fact that each had loved someone else before. They both knew and understood.

They talked for a long time, about other things, and it was good sitting there with him, seeing the stars in the sky and hearing the evening breeze rustling the palm fronds. It was after ten when she got up to leave.

Tokay! Tokay! came the loud cry of a lizard. Rae counted the cries. 'Only six,' she said, when the reptile was silent. 'He's not in great shape.'

Jason laughed and came to his feet, too, reaching for her hands. 'Come here,' he ordered softly. He drew her into his arms. 'Thanks for coming.'

'I wanted to.' She looked into his eyes, her blood rushing fast through her veins.

'I'm always thinking about you lately,' he said. 'I keep wanting to kiss you.'

She gave him a taunting smile. 'Then why don't you?'

'You think I should ask for permission first?'

'You should, yes. In writing, in triplicate, notarised. Then you get a licence with a stamp on it and an identification card with your picture on it, and you need to show that every time you want to kiss.'

'And what if I don't have one?' His gaze lingered on her lips and she felt small delicious bubbles of excitement rise to her head like golden champagne.

'They'll arrest you and throw you in gaol for life.'

He grinned. 'Oh, well, what the hell? It's worth the risk.'

He drew her against him and she closed her eyes as she felt the firm warmth of his mouth on her lips. Her pulse leaped and the champagne bubbles exploded in her head and all was sweetness and magic. Her mouth opened eagerly to his and he gave a low groan in his throat. There was a hungering wildness, as if something had broken loose inside them. Kisses—frenzied kisses, deep, yearning kisses. She clung to him, arms around his neck, fingers in his hair, lost in the shivering sensations sweeping over her.

His body suddenly grew rigid against her. He drew back abruptly and her trembling body screamed in protest. She opened her eyes, seeing Anouk standing in the door leading to the veranda. In her long white nightgown, her curly hair like a halo around her head, she looked like a red-haired angel in the shadowed darkness of the night.

She stared at the two of them for an endless moment, but Rae couldn't read the expression on the small white face. Then, without a word, Anouk turned and ran back inside.

'Oh, damn!' Jason muttered. He drew her face against his shoulder. 'I'm sorry. I'd better go and see her.'

Rae's heart sank. 'You think she's upset?'

He let go of her and sighed wearily. 'I have no idea.' He raked his hand through his hair. 'I'm sorry.'

'So am I.' She bit her lip. 'I'd better go now.'

'If you don't mind waiting, I'll walk you home.'

'You're expecting a phone call from the States.'

He frowned irritably. 'Damn, yes.'

She touched his hand. 'It doesn't matter.'

'Will you be all right?'

'Of course I will. This is not New York.'

She walked home, down the hill, past the other houses in the dark street. A dog barked at her through a closed gate. A watchman wished her *selamat malam* in a slow, lazy drawl. The air felt warm and muggy and it seemed hard to breathe. She wished the evening could have ended on a happier note. She wished she knew what to do about Anouk.

* * *

An idea was taking shape in her head. She mulled it over all the next day, then went to see Hillie.

'I'd like you to teach me some Dutch. I don't mean the language, but just a few lines.' She handed Hillie a sheet of paper and she glanced over it quickly.

'You don't give up easily, do you?' Hillie asked.

'We've got to do something.'

'Yes, I know. What do you think she'll do when you say this to her?'

'I have no idea. I'm just thinking. . .I. . .maybe it's all wrong, but I think that to Anouk Dutch is much more than just the language she speaks; she associates it with her mother, her father, her grandparents. It means love, happiness, security, everything that's familiar. She likes to be at your house because it feels like home to her. First she had to deal with her mother's death. Then Jason moved here, taking her away from everything that meant home and security. I think normally, as in your case, the whole family moves, but Anouk was already dealing with the loss of her mother, and then the other separation on top of it caused something to go wrong.' She looked at Hillie. 'Do I sound like I'm nuts?'

'No, go on.'

'Jason demands that she learn English. When he speaks it to her, she becomes hysterical and she cries herself to sleep. It's another loss, you see. When he speaks English he isn't the same familiar father—he's like a stranger. I think it's all related to that, somehow. Does it make sense?'

Hillie nodded slowly. 'Absolutely. I think you've got it. English is a threat to her because it symbolises a loss of love or something like that.'

'I think so.'

Hillie looked down at the paper. 'Well, let's give this a try.' She looked up and grinned. 'Repeat after me: *Je moet eens goed naar me luisteren.*'

Rae groaned, dropping her head in defeat. 'I give up,' she said.

Hillie laughed. 'No, you won't. Shall I get us a pot of tea?'

'You're as bad as the English. They think tea is a solution for everything.'

'It's a miracle potion. It even helps you to speak Dutch, you will see.'

'I think it will take something more like a bottle of Scotch.'

Rae practised all weekend, calling Hillie on the phone a couple of times, and stopping by on Monday for further intensive training. By Tuesday Hillie was satisfied that Rae had mastered the few sentences she'd intended to learn.

That same afternoon Rae called Jason to see if she could come over and see Anouk. Walking up to the familiar house, she saw Anouk playing soccer with the boys next door, calling out to them in Indonesian, laughing at their answers. She wondered if these little Indonesian boys didn't find it beneath their male dignity to play soccer with a mere girl. When Anouk caught sight of Rae she stopped and stared at her for a moment, then demonstratively turned her back.

I'm the enemy, Rae thought sadly. The big gates were wide open and she walked up to the house. Jason himself opened the door to let her in.

'Hi.' He wore khaki shorts and a white shirt, and the familiar thrill went through her as his eyes met hers.

'Hi,' she answered, stepping past him. He reached out and drew her to him.

'Not so fast,' he said in her ear, and kissed her quickly. 'I know it's not me you wanted to see, but I can have a mere minute, can't I?'

She smiled at him sunnily. 'I know better than to come between a man and his work. How are your Washington friends doing?'

'Complaining about the hotel, the food, the weather, the people. They've got lizards in their rooms, the steaks are tough, the weather is too muggy, the people aren't American.' He rolled his eyes in exasperation. 'I'll be more than ready for a lazy weekend in Sarangan next week. So where is my daughter?'

As he spoke the words, Anouk came into the entrance.

'Mrs Smith wants to talk to you,' Jason said in English. 'I'll be in my office if you need me.'

They went into the living-room. 'Let's sit down here,' Rae suggested. She lowered herself on to the sofa and patted the seat next to her. Anouk sat down, as far away from her as possible.

Rae ached to touch her, to hold her and wipe away the anger and hurt on the small face. She took a deep breath, hoping that maybe her efforts would break down some of the barriers.

'Anouk,' she began slowly, '*je moet eens goed naar me luisteren.*' She went on, speaking the unfamiliar words carefully. 'I know you are sad about your mother, and you miss your grandparents.' As she spoke, she looked at the bent head. It shot up suddenly, eyes wide with shock, the face deathly pale. Anouk jumped up from the sofa, body rigid, hands clenched into fists.

'You are not my mother!' she shouted in English. 'You are not my mother! Don't talk to me like that! I don't want to hear it!' Her voice, high with anger, broke. Tears rolled down her face and the small body trembled.

Rigid with shock, Rae stared at the girl, then instinctively reached out to take her in her arms, wanting to comfort her, dry the tears. Anouk struggled wildly, sobbing miserably, but Rae held on to her.

'It's all right, Anouk,' she said calmly, holding her firmly. 'It's all right. I am not your mother. I know that. All I want is for you to be happy. We all want you to be happy.'

'That is not true! You. . .my father. . .you want that I speak English!'

'It's only for school and for your English friends. Dutch is for your home. You can talk Dutch with your father and with your Dutch friends.'

'But not you! I don't want that you talk Dutch to me! Only my mother and my father and my. . .*opa* and *oma*. Not you!' There was amazing strength in the wiry body, and she freed herself from Rae's grip. She jumped away from the sofa, glaring at Rae with tear-filled eyes. 'You are not my mother!'

Behind Anouk's back, a movement caught Rae's eye. Jason stood in the door, silently, watching the two of them. She wondered how long he had been standing there and her stomach churned with anxiety. Oh, God, she'd made a mess of things. After all the silent defiance from Anouk, she had not expected this emotional outburst. And certainly not one in English.

Anouk took one swift look at her father and ran up the stairs. Jason advanced into the room, his face a mask of anger. He stood in front of Rae, looming large overhead.

'What the hell do you think you're doing?' he asked, in a voice so coldly furious that it chilled her to the bone.

Her tongue lay paralysed in her mouth. She closed her eyes and swallowed hard.

'I tried. . .I just wanted to try this one thing. . .' Her voice trailed away.

He stood perfectly still, his big body rigid with restrained fury, his eyes like chips of blue ice.

'Aren't you the one who told me you are a teacher, not a therapist?' His voice cut the air like a knife. 'Will you please keep your experiments within the realm of teaching?'

For a moment indignation fought her despair. He
had no right to treat her as if she were some irrespon-
sible nut. She clenched her hands. 'I wanted to help. I
just wanted to help!'

'Obviously, you didn't!' he bit out, turning on his
heel and making for the stairs.

She shrank from his tone, the look in his eyes. She
watched his back as he took the stairs two at a time.
She was shaking, her nerves shattered. She could not
believe this was happening to her; she could not believe
the cold anger she had seen in his eyes. She shivered
convulsively. The terrible thing was that Jason was
right. She was not a psychologist and she shouldn't
have played with his daughter's head. At least she
should have discussed her idea with Jason first.

Yet what she had said had not been that perturbing
or upsetting. Anouk's reaction, she was sure, had not
been because of the words. It had been caused by the
fact that Rae had spoken them in Dutch.

And she had done it to create an atmosphere of
intimacy and closeness, to take away Anouk's fear and
sense of threat, to gain her trust.

It had worked entirely the opposite way. She covered
her face with her hands and moaned.

She sat like that for what seemed like a long time,
and finally she raised her head, wiping her hair out of
her face. It was very quiet in the house, the air heavy
with damp and doom. She struggled to her feet. She
had to go. She didn't want to be here when Jason came
back down; she'd seen enough of his anger to last her
a lifetime. She winced, remembering his voice, his
eyes. Oh, God, she didn't want to see him look at her
like that ever again.

She walked down the hill in a daze, wishing this
whole day would just go away, wishing she had never
had the stupid idea of talking to Anouk in Dutch.

Jason would never forgive her for upsetting his daughter. Despite the heat, she felt chilled to the bone.

There were people at the house when she came back and she joined them on the veranda, grateful for the diversion. She needed something to make the nightmare go away—laughter, talk. Something so that she wouldn't feel the cold despair settling inside her.

Later they all went out to dinner in the Chinese part of town, to a small restaurant with chipped formica tables, a dog asleep in the corner and the most delicious food.

It was late when they finally came back. Rae went to her room, showered and pulled on a nightgown. She sat up in bed and tried to read. She knew she couldn't sleep; her head was too busy with the incident of the afternoon. Jason's anger was still with her, like an icy hand clutching her heart.

She heard noises outside on the veranda. Footsteps. She held her breath and listened. Maybe it was the watchman making his rounds. Only he had seemed quite asleep when they'd come back from the restaurant.

There was a knock on the veranda door. 'Rae?'

Her heart jumped into her throat. She swung her legs out of bed and opened the door.

'Jason?' It was past twelve. What was he doing here in the middle of the night?

He raked his hands through his hair. He looked dishevelled in the pale moonlight. 'I'm sorry,' he said. 'I didn't want to come to the front door and wake Nicky and David.'

She swallowed. 'Why are you here?' She didn't want to hear more accusations, although he didn't seem angry, just tired. His eyes were clouded and lines of fatigue ran along his mouth.

'I called all night and no one answered. I came by

several times and no one was home. I'm sorry it's so late, but I need to talk to you. Can I come in?'

She hesitated, then moved aside, closing the door behind him.

'How's Anouk?' she asked, afraid to hear the answer, yet needing to know.

'She's fine.'

She looked at him squarely and steeled herself. She would apologise for making a mistake, but she wouldn't let him think he had been justified in saying what he had said to her. 'Jason, I'm sorry,' she said calmly. 'I didn't mean to upset Anouk like that. I thought if I talked to her in Dutch it would make her trust me more. I realise I should not have——'

He shook his head to stop her words. 'Rae, I'm the one to apologise. I don't know what came over me. All I saw was Anouk and that look in her eyes. I can't believe the things I said to you.'

She searched his face, relief washing over her. He was no longer angry. He had come to Anouk's rescue like a mother lion defending her cub. The image of Jason as a mother lion made her smile inwardly. 'I wasn't too crazy about what you said, either,' she admitted.

He looked pained. 'Don't hate me.'

'I don't hate you.'

His eyes held hers. 'That's good.'

She sighed. 'I shouldn't have done what I did. Or at least I should have talked it over with you first.' She sat down on the edge of the bed. 'I had no idea she would react the way she did. She has always refused to talk to me.'

'Maybe it was exactly what she needed.'

Rae frowned, not comprehending. 'What do you mean?'

'It's the first time she's really talked to me since we came here.' He rubbed his forehead as if to push away the weariness. 'There was so much bottled up, and she wouldn't let go. She wouldn't tell me what she was thinking and feeling. I think we made progress today. She said again that she wants to go back to Holland. I had to explain to her that it isn't possible, so we compromised.' His smile held a touch of defeat. 'I will not speak English to her any more, except when we're with someone else who doesn't speak Dutch, and we'll see if we can get her grandparents to come here to visit.'

Rae nodded. 'Sounds like a good idea. I think she misses them. Maybe it will help.'

He paced the room restlessly. 'I shouldn't have involved you in my problem. It was my problem all along and I made it yours.'

'I'm her teacher. How can I not be involved? I want to help her, Jason, I really do.'

'I know, and you did. Let's see what happens now. Play it by ear.'

She nodded. 'OK.' She stared at her hands in her lap, hesitating. 'She said I'm not her mother. Where did that come from?'

'She saw us kissing. And then when you started speaking Dutch to her you were suddenly much too close for comfort.'

Her chest felt tight. 'She hates me,' she said tonelessly.

He moved over to the bed and sat down next to her. 'I don't think so, not deep down. She needed somebody to blame and you were handy.'

She sighed. 'Oh, Jason, I wish I could have handled this better. I didn't think——'

He put his arm around her. 'Rae, it's all right. Please don't beat yourself. She talked to me, for the first time in months. It's progress, and sometimes progress is painful.' He paused. 'As it seems to be between you and me. I'm sorry, Rae, for what I said this afternoon. I wasn't myself.'

His blue gaze held hers and a warm lightness filled her and made her smile. 'I'll forgive you if you'll forgive me.'

Laughter shone in his eyes. 'It's a deal.' He wrapped his arms around her and leaned his face towards her. 'I'm going to kiss you,' he whispered. 'And you'd better be prepared. It's going to be the best kiss you've ever had in your life. It'll knock your socks off.'

She gave a smothered laugh. 'I'm not wearing——'

She had no time to finish her sentence. No time for anything except the sudden fierce pressure of his mouth on hers. No more laughing now, no more jokes. A wild, wondrous sense of longing unfolded inside her like a red jungle flower. He drew her down with him on to the bed. His mouth explored hers, his tongue tempting, tantalising. She felt a breathless desire to be closer yet, and she brushed against him with fluid urgency, moulding herself to him. He withdrew slightly, sliding his hand between their bodies, cupping her breast. There was only the thin covering of cotton and she felt her breast surge and swell in his big, warm hand. His thumb touched her nipple and sparks of fire, almost painful, shot through her. A moan escaped her, and he withdrew his hand. 'Jason. . .' She was trembling, or was it him? She wanted him close to her, she wanted his hand on her body. She wanted, wanted. . .

He lay still, his face against her breast, and she could feel his breath on her skin. He was breathing hard, his body rigid with utter control.

'Jason?'

He shook his head, then suddenly sat up, raking both hands through his hair. She watched him, heart pounding, as he sat there, his head bent. She wanted to reach out and pull him back down to her. *No*, she thought. No. Not so soon, not so easily.

Finally he came slowly to his feet. He looked down
at her as she still lay on the bed, his eyes a stormy blue.
Then he leaned down and kissed her gently. 'That
wasn't what I came here for tonight,' he said softly,
'but don't think for a minute that I don't want you.'

He moved over to the veranda door, and Rae sat up,
wiping the hair out of her eyes. 'Jason?'

He turned to look at her. 'Yes?'

'Why did you come tonight? Why didn't you wait till
tomorrow?' Why did she ask the question? She already
knew the answer.

'I felt. . .bad,' he said on a low note. He paused
fractionally. 'I don't like going to sleep feeling something is wrong. I had to make it right.'

One of the agreements he had lived by in his
marriage, no doubt, as she had in hers. Never go to
bed angry or upset.

'I'm glad,' she said softly.

He smiled. 'Goodnight, Rae.' He opened the door
quietly and slipped away from her into the warm, dark
night.

The next morning Anouk came into the classroom,
pushed her desk back in its original place and sat down,
looking defiantly at the other children, daring them to
say anything. Nobody did.

Anouk was learning English, and she was ahead of
everybody. She seemed determined that, if she was
going to speak English, she was going to do it better
than everybody else in the class. Rae smiled inwardly
as she watched Anouk take charge of herself.

She still wasn't happy. Rae understood well enough
what was going on. They had an unspoken pact: Anouk
would speak English if Rae would not speak Dutch.

CHAPTER FIVE

'You want to ride with us to Sarangan?' Jason asked her the next day.

She wanted nothing more, but she shook her head regretfully. 'I think it would be better not, Jason. I'm not sure Anouk will appreciate spending four hours with me in a car.'

'Miranda is riding with us. The two will be in the back and they won't even notice us.'

She hesitated. 'Are you sure?'

'I'm very sure. I'm not crazy about spending all that time with two giggly six-year-olds. If she can have a friend, so can I.' There was undisguised humour in his eyes.

Friend. Was that what she was? She thought of the night before, the long breathless kisses as they had lain on her bed, his hands touching her.

'All right, then, I'd like to come with you.'

'Good.' His gaze held hers, and she noticed the dark gleam in his eyes, a wordless message that made her heart skip a beat.

They left soon after lunch on Friday in Jason's personal car, a comfortable Toyota sedan that came equipped with the luxury of air-conditioning. The two girls had settled themselves in the back with their toys. They whispered and giggled, looking at Dutch comic books, or playing games with Barbie dolls. They seemed totally engrossed in their own activities, paying no attention to the two adults in the front as they proceeded down the road out of town.

Jason threw her a quick glance, blue eyes laughing.

'See? I told you.' He took his hand off the wheel and touched hers briefly. 'I'm glad you're coming with us.'

She felt a delicious sense of anticipation about the weekend, a quivering excitement in the pit of her stomach. I'm like a teenager in love, she thought, and she smiled inwardly. Only she was not a teenager, but a grown woman. She knew what it all meant, what the risks and consequences could be of those combustible feelings, and it wasn't something to take lightly.

The road out of Semarang was narrow and crowded with traffic: huge buses thundering by at death-defying speed, painted trucks groaning under heavy loads, squeaky carts struggling along pulled by oxen or horses. The road wound through bustling towns and villages, past colourful markets and houses painted pink and green.

They talked easily, and Rae watched Jason as he drove the car expertly through the busy traffic, avoiding motorcycles, people and assorted wildlife that ventured out on to the road. He exuded an air of quiet competence and his calm, sure manner instilled in her a sense of trust and confidence. You could find yourself stranded in the middle of the desert with this man and he'd get you out. Alive. The thought made her smile. She was falling for this man in no uncertain way, and she wanted it to happen. She didn't want to worry about it or be distrustful. She just wanted it to happen.

He looked at her suddenly, as if he'd felt her watching him. 'What are you smiling about?' he asked, and for a moment she struggled to find something to say before she blushed like a teenager.

'Deserts,' she said.

'Deserts?' Laughing lights danced in his eyes. 'That makes sense, sure. Do you often think of deserts?'

'All the time. Don't you?'

'Actually, no.'

'Deserts are interesting. Sand, rock, cactuses.'

'Cacti,' he corrected.

She made a face. 'I knew that. I was just testing you.'

Farther east the road turned narrower yet and the activity slowed down. The scenery offered breathtaking vistas of green hills, terraced rice paddies in luscious jewel-green, a glorious blue sky. Picturesque villages huddled in the shade of coconut palms. Chickens ran for safety, squawking hysterically as the car approached. There were goats and ducks and cowardly dogs, and everywhere children with large dark eyes played by the road and waved as they passed.

In the back seat the girls had fallen asleep, faces tucked into small pillows resting against the windows. Rae glanced back and smiled. They looked so sweet and innocent, both of them. They were quite a pair, the little blonde and the red-head, but not always innocent and angelic when they conspired against Sander who, despite his age and size, was not always prepared for their tricks.

Jason's blue eyes caught hers when she straightened in her seat. 'You love kids, don't you?' he asked.

She nodded. 'When I was little I said I was going to have five of them.'

He whistled softly. 'Very brave.'

'I was very little,' she said drily.

'And now? How many would you like now?'

'I'm not thinking in numbers any more. I'll be glad to have one before I'm too old.'

He laughed. 'You're not exactly over the hill yet, are you?'

'I'm twenty-seven and single. It's not promising in terms of motherhood.'

He focused on the road in front of him. 'You don't need a husband to have a child.'

'I do.' She glanced at him, wondering if he was testing her.

He met her eyes and a slow smile curved his mouth. 'Old-fashioned, are you?'

She shrugged. 'I don't know if that's it. I just don't see myself as a single mother. Now my friend Kate, she's got it all planned out. The day she turns thirty, married or not, she's going to try and have a baby. But I'd just as soon have my kid have a father and me a husband. It's cosier that way.'

'Cosy? That's a nice way of saying it. And yes, you're right.'

'Don't let my friend Kate hear it. She'd have a fit. She thinks I'm much too romantic and idealistic. She's a terrible cynic, although at times she regresses into hopefulness.'

'I take it she's not married.'

'She's much too picky and demanding, I'm afraid.'

'And you're not?'

'Oh, I am, on certain points, but who's perfect? My marriage taught me a lot.' She gave a half smile. 'Even my husband wasn't perfect.' Matt had been hopelessly sloppy, leaving his clothes all over the floor, never picking up after himself, smoking a pack of cigarettes a day. She'd hated the smoking, the smell in the house, on the curtains, the carpets. She'd dreaded thinking what it was doing to his lungs.

'Even your husband,' he repeated. 'Sounds like he was quite a man.'

'Oh, he was.' She fell silent and he gave her a quick, sideways glance.

'Go on,' he urged.

She shook her head, feeling awkward. What was she supposed to tell him? That Matt had been handsome, highly intelligent, charming? That she had loved him to distraction? She was in love with Jason now, and she wasn't sure how to talk to him about Matt.

He did not insist. 'On what points are you picky and demanding?' he asked when she remained silent.

'In terms of relationships with men?'

'Right.'

She gave him a taunting smile. 'I suppose you might as well know. Just in case.'

His mouth quirked. 'Just in case.'

She straightened in her seat. 'I want a wealthy man, someone very handsome and powerful. I want a house on the beach in California and apartments in New York and Paris, and he has to be passionately in love with me and be faithful for the rest of our lives.'

He let out a deep sigh. 'I'm afraid I'm not your man.'

'I could compromise,' she said promptly. 'Forget the apartment in New York. Who needs New York?'

He gave a hearty laugh. Amazingly, the girls did not wake up. He reached out and took her hand. 'Now tell me what you really want. Somehow you don't strike me as a woman who's terribly interested in money and fancy houses. Coming to Java certainly isn't giving you that. Westchester County would have been a better bet.' His hand let go of hers and moved back to the steering-wheel.

She hesitated, feeling suddenly uncertain and vulnerable. It was easy to joke and make light of things, but giving away how she really felt and what she truly wanted was risky. She stole a glance at him. He was looking at the road and not at her, but he was waiting for an answer.

'I want love,' she said. 'The whole package—honesty, fidelity, trust.'

He gave her a quick, sideways glance. 'High standards,' he said evenly.

'It's the only way to live. It's not such a nice world out there. You need a home base where you're always safe—a person who loves and accepts you unconditionally.'

'Yes.' His eyes did not leave the road. Then he smiled. 'What does your friend Kate think of that?'

'Oh, she thinks I'm much too naïve. No man can stay faithful for any length of time in her opinion.' She studied his face. 'What do you think?'

'About being faithful? I was married for over six years. I had no trouble whatsoever being faithful to my wife.'

There was no doubt in her mind that he was telling the truth. 'You loved your wife, didn't you?' she asked, her voice low, afraid suddenly that she shouldn't have asked. But he wasn't offended.

'Yes, I did, Rae.'

They were silent for a while, absorbed in their own thoughts as they drove on. When the girls awoke they stopped for a soft drink in a tiny *warung*, then continued on the slowly climbing road to Tawangmangu, a small hill town full of white-painted guest-houses. It was too high now for rice, and plots of cabbage, maize and other vegetables hugged the rolling hills in a colourful patchwork design. The colours were bright and clear in the cool clean air, and Jason turned off the air-conditioning and opened the windows.

'It feels great,' Rae said, taking in a deep breath.

'Tired yet?' he asked.

She shook her head. How can I be tired when I'm sitting next to you? she asked silently. She was much too aware of him, of his eyes and his voice, to feel anything but very alive and very awake.

In the back seat Barbie was going to the doctor. It was easy to guess from the secretive giggles and the word 'doctor' that Rae kept hearing amid the tumble of incomprehensible Dutch, and the fact that Barbie was being divested of all her clothes.

Jason glanced in the rear-view mirror, apparently surveying the goings-on in the back, then grinned at Rae. 'At least they're using the right words,' he said on a low note.

She felt so good sitting here next to him, watching

his hands on the wheel, listening to his voice as he told her stories about other times and other places. She thought of how it would be if she spent the rest of her life with him, having children, a family. Then a cloud cooled her fantasies as she thought of Anouk. Anouk might never accept her.

She stared out of the window, seeing two small boys carrying enormous loads of rattan baskets on their shoulders, and in the distance now she saw the high peaks of the mountains shrouded in clouds. The road grew steeper and steeper and the views more spectacular with every turn.

She thought of Jason's wife, with whom he must have planned a future, and she thought of Matt and the dreams they'd had. For a moment there was sadness, then the fierce wish that the past should not intrude on the present. No thoughts now of lost dreams, but of other dreams to come. She stole a look at Jason, who concentrated on the narrow, curving road, and felt a surge of exhilaration, of sweet anticipation. This weekend would be special.

Forests, primeval and dense, replaced the cultivated hills. They'd seen not a single car in the last twenty minutes, and it seemed they were alone in this silent, misty world of ancient trees, green lichen and moss-covered rocks. They groped their way over the mountain ridge and back down the other side, and the wild and unspoiled landscape stirred in her an answering, primitive feeling, a secret longing.

Out of the forest, the road crawled down, through greening hills and market gardens, twisting and turning sharply until finally the white-painted buildings of Sarangan came into view.

The hotel was a two-storey building with rooms overlooking the small lake with its magnificent backdrop of wooded mountains.

'This is glorious,' Rae said as she got out of the car.

She stretched, reaching her arms high above her head, trying to touch the cool blue sky. She inhaled the fragrant air and slowly let it out. 'Paradise.' She caught Jason's amused smile as he watched her and dropped her arms self-consciously.

The children scrambled out of the back seat and took off like arrows from a bow, in search of friends who had arrived earlier. The Moermans were already there, as were Josie and Steve plus baby Rosalie and several others.

A young man in a red T-shirt helped them take their suitcases to the rooms, which were on the same level, but separated by a number of others. A wide gallery ran along the front of all the rooms, with outside chairs and tables for relaxing and enjoying the view. There were flowers everywhere, window-boxes and large planters full of trailing petunias in every possible shade, and vivid pink and red geraniums. It was a lovely place, although the rooms were modest and the furniture old and a bit shabby. There was a fireplace in every room and big, soft beds with faded, flowered bedspreads.

A young girl with smiling dark eyes brought pots of tea and small snacks which she placed on the tables outside.

'Tea at my place?' Rae offered, and Jason settled himself in one of the baby-blue painted chairs, stretching his legs.

'What I should do is have a run around the lake to get my system moving again. But first I'll have tea.' He grinned. 'I've become irredeemably Europeanised, I'm afraid—at least where it concerns afternoon tea. Do you know that many offices have tea ladies, or coffee girls as they call them in Holland? Mid-morning they make the rounds with a tea trolley and give everybody coffee, and in the afternoon everyone gets tea. No brewing your own whenever you feel like it. It was a little hard getting used to.'

'You should feel at home here,' Rae said, as she filled the cups. Hailing back to colonial times, the place had a distinctly European touch with its flowers and tea and cool, clean air.

Enjoying the little domestic scene, Rae sipped her tea and surveyed the surroundings. 'It feels like spring here,' she said.

His eyes, blue as the sky, smiled into hers. 'It does, doesn't it?' There was a deeper meaning in the simple words and it amazed her how he could reach into her heart with just a few words, or just the tone of his voice or the look in his eyes.

Later there was a communal meal in the hotel dining-room: beef, boiled potatoes, green beans and gravy, preceded with light vegetables soup and followed by a custard pudding. It was a decidedly uninspired meal with no sign of anything Indonesian, intended to please the western palates, which weren't pleased. The cook, too, hailed back to colonial times, ancient and wrinkled and over-polite.

After dinner, they joined Nicky and David and a few others in front of a huge crackling fire in the hotel lounge and played cards, but by nine o'clock Rae couldn't keep her eyes open any longer. Maybe it was the fire that made her drowsy, or maybe the pure mountain air had gone straight to her head, she wasn't sure.

Jason walked her back to her room and the cold air revived her somewhat. The night was glorious, with more stars than she had ever seen. Jason kissed her goodnight in front of her door, a long, dizzying kiss that held a wealth of meaning, yet she felt the restraint in him, and when he withdrew he smiled at her ruefully.

'I'd better get back to my room and check up on Anouk,' he said.

Despite her fatigue, she felt a stab of disappointment. This was not a night to be alone. She wanted to hold on to him and ask him to stay with her, but she knew he would not leave his daughter alone in the room for the night.

Still, despite the too-soft mattress and the restlessness of her body, she slept long and deeply, waking to a cold, sunny morning with the mist swirling around the mountain peaks.

It was a good day, filled with activities and cool, clean air. In the morning Rae walked around the lake with part of the group, while the more fanatic Hash House Harrier runners, which included Jason, went on a tortuous run up into the mountains, following a trail of shredded paper laid the day before by some of the runners. In the afternoon, Rae declined Jason's invitation to join him and Anouk for a boat ride on the lake. She didn't want to intrude too much on the father-daughter relationship.

Instead, she went to the village market with Nicky to look around and to take pictures. She enjoyed being with Nicky and her infectious enthusiasm for everything—colours and shapes and the play of light. She photographed children, little old ladies, the colourful boats on the lake, the vegetables heaped in the market.

In the evening there was more talking and playing of games as everyone huddled in their jeans and sweaters. By ten everyone was still going strong, aided by beer and wine, but Rae had had enough. She glanced around the room, seeing Jason playing chess with Joost, frowning in concentration. He looked up suddenly, as if he had sensed that she was watching him. His eyes locked with hers for a moment, then he looked back at the board.

Rae escaped the warm lobby and slowly walked around the grounds. The lake was very smooth and the moon was reflected in the dark water. Beyond lay the mountains, dotted with lights at the lower slopes. Rae leaned against the railing of the gallery in front of her room and surveyed the peaceful scene, inhaling the cool, cedar-scented air. Crickets filled the night with their chirping, and she smiled at nothing in particular. It felt good, just for a little while, to be away from the noise and laughter of the group.

Rae couldn't help noticing, with everybody so close all day, the togetherness of families and couples. It made her feel lonely and left out, which was really quite unnecessary. Nobody excluded her directly or indirectly, but there were times like these when she missed being part of a couple, having someone to share her life with. A sense of melancholy overwhelmed her.

She noticed someone approaching in the dark, seeing, as he came closer, that it was Jason.

'Hello, Rae,' he said, standing next to her. 'Haven't seen much of you today.'

'No.'

In the pale light of the moon he scrutinised her face.

'Are you all right?' he asked.

'I'm fine,' she answered, feeling vulnerable under his probing eyes.

His gaze held hers for a moment, and her heart began to beat erratically. Then he leaned his arms on the rail and looked out over the water. For a while they stood together in silence. She wondered what he was thinking, if he missed his wife on beautiful, romantic nights such as this.

'Ah, such quiet,' he said at last. He turned his head and smiled at her. 'Did the jollying get to you?'

'It was getting a little wild. I just felt like being alone for a while. It's so beautiful here.'

'Would you like me to leave?'

'No.' She smiled. 'Just don't start singing bawdy drinking songs.'

He laughed softly. 'It's a deal.'

'Who won the chess game?'

'Joost.' His tone held amusement.

'That should make him happy. Hillie told me you almost always win when you play together.'

'I'm not so sure he's happy.'

'Why not?'

'His luck changed dramatically after I saw you leave and he knew why.'

Rae laughed. 'You let him win?'

'Not really. Let's just say my concentration was gone and I wanted to have it over with as fast as possible so I could come after you.'

'You're a bad sport.'

'Terrible, indeed,' he agreed. 'Just don't tell Anouk, or I'll come crashing down off my pedestal.

Rae laughed. Anouk, she would bet, would never let anybody win, no matter what the reason. 'Is she asleep?' she asked.

'I doubt it.' His tone held amusement. 'She's staying with the Moerman clan. They have one of those dormitory rooms and they invited her to spend the night with them. She was ecstatic, of course.' The corner of his mouth quirked. 'A sole father is pretty dull company.'

His voice was even, yet she sensed the pain behind the words. Besides losing his wife, he'd also lost the mother of his child. Had she lived, there might have been a brother or a sister now. A real family.

She shivered in the cold air, hugging herself, feeling sadness for him, for herself. For all the losses and pain. 'Who would ever think it could get so cold in the tropics?' she asked, hoping her voice would not betray her feelings.

'It seems strange.' He gazed over the water, still leaning against the railing. 'If you'd like,' he said very quietly, 'I could keep you warm tonight.'

Her heart seemed to stop. She swallowed, not looking at him. It was a simple offer, one she could very easily refuse. And he had meant it to be so. He was not touching her; he hadn't even looked at her as he'd spoken the words. He knew as well as she did that if he held her and kissed her, she would have no choice. He knew too well how she reacted to his touch. He wanted an answer made with her head as well as her heart.

A lump lodged in her throat. It would have been so easy for him to get her into bed if that was all he wanted. But he wasn't just thinking of himself, and his selfless caring was like a gift of love.

She longed to feel his warmth and the strength of his body. It had been so long since she had felt the comfort of arms around her in the night. She longed to hold him and give him herself. She reached out and touched his hand where it lay on the railing and his fingers curled around hers.

'I think,' she heard herself say, 'that it would be better if we kept each other warm.'

CHAPTER SIX

RAE saw Jason smile, and then she was in his arms, her face against the soft wool of his sweater.

'I'd like that,' he said, and there was an odd tone to his voice. 'I'd like that much better.'

He lifted her face to his and she closed her eyes, feeling his lips on hers, his mouth warm and hungry. All sadness left her and warmth flowed through her body, chasing the cold and leaving her trembling with longing. She clung to him, responding to his kisses with a reckless abandon.

'Your place or mine?' he whispered, and the frivolity of the question made her laugh.

'What's the difference?'

'I've got a fire ready to light in mine.'

'Your place, then.' She withdrew slightly. 'Give me twenty minutes, and I'll be there.'

He brushed his lips across hers. 'Make it fifteen.'

'I'll try,' she whispered.

He hugged her tightly, then released her. 'Go, and be quick.'

She was. Seventeen minutes later she stood in front of his door and knocked, her heart fluttering crazily in her throat.

The room was toasty warm, and lit only by the fire and a couple of stubby white candles supplied by the hotel in case the electricity failed. The electricity, however, had not failed, and Rae smiled at Jason as he let her in.

'This is so romantic.'

'We try,' he said with a half smile. 'Anything to obscure the décor.'

101

'I like it. It's romantically shabby. Especially by candle-light.'

He drew her into his arms and held her tight, as if he were afraid she would escape. 'Look what else I have.' He nodded at the table next to the bed and she saw a bottle of wine catching the light from the fire.

'Where did you get that?'

'I stole it. From Kevin. He has a case of it sitting in his room, and the whole gang was drinking beer and playing poker.'

Rae gave a smothered laugh. 'I thought you were an honest man.'

His lips gently bit her earlobe. 'I'm just trying to help out. Don't want him to think nobody wants his Australian wine.'

'I'd like some.'

'You can have some.' His hands moved to her front and unzipped her jacket, then slipped it off her shoulders. Strangely, it seemed an intimate gesture, even though it was nothing more than a jacket and she was still wearing a sweater and a shirt underneath.

He poured wine into two water glasses. 'Sorry, no goblets.'

'Who needs goblets?' She sat down on the little rug in front of the fire and he sat next to her, raising his glass to hers. 'To a warm night,' he said softly, smiling into her eyes. Her heart made a dizzy little leap and she couldn't take her gaze away, watching the reflection of the fire in his eyes.

They sipped the wine slowly. His hand was in her hair, fingers playing with the curls, and she sat very still, feeling the warmth curling in the centre of her body. His hands, very lightly, moved forward, tracing her jaw, then with a feathery touch trailed down her throat, and lower, until it gently rested on her left breast.

It was hard to swallow, hard to breathe. She stared

into the flames, feeling the heat of his hand through her clothes. Then, slowly, very slowly, his hand moved down her stomach and on to her jean-covered thigh and lay there.

'Rae?'

She looked at him, seeing his face, all light and shadows in the golden glow of the leaping flames of the fire. He took her hand.

'We have to be practical for a moment,' he said softly. 'I don't want to take for granted that you took care of that. If you like——'

She shook her head. 'No, it's all right. I took care of it.'

'Sure?'

She nodded. 'Thank you for asking.'

He put his glass down and slipped his arms around her. She closed her eyes as his mouth found hers.

He began to undress her slowly, kissing her with tantalising little kisses. She savoured the anticipation, the mounting tension. Her skin tingled with his touch, her body glowed with life. She slipped her hands over his body, yearning to feel his warm skin, the strong muscles of his arms and chest—all of him.

His slow, unhurried movements did not deceive her. He was taking his time to lengthen the sweet torture, stirring in her a restless fever. He kissed her breasts, and they tingled with life, eager for his touch. She moved her hands under his sweater and shirt, to find the warm skin of his chest and back.

He raised her to her feet and held her close, and she felt his body's response against her. He slipped off her jeans and panties, sliding them down her legs, and she felt a weakness invade her, a fever stirring her blood. His clothes followed hers to the floor, not with slow deliberation, but with determined haste.

The breath stuck in her throat at the sight of the male beauty of his naked body, the play of shadows of the leaping fire on his brown skin. His eyes gleamed darkly into hers, then slowly looked over her body, his gaze like a caress. His hand began to trail a path down her arms, her hips, back up over her stomach to her breasts.

'Do you know how much I've wanted to see you and touch you?' he said huskily, moving her over to the bed. 'Do you know how much I want you?'

'No,' she whispered, shaken by the fire in his eyes, the hunger in his voice.

'I'll show you.'

They lay down on the bed, arms around each other, mouths and bodies clinging. She closed her eyes and sighed, revelling in his nearness, glorying in the warmth of the strong, muscled body touching hers. She felt heady with a delicious excitement, like a bubbly champagne warming her blood.

And he began to show her—with his hands, with his mouth, his body. He showed her with gentleness and skill, with fervour and passion, until her body and mind were lost in a sea of sensual delight. There was only his body and hers, joined together in an ancient ritual of love and passion.

Desire leaped like the flames of the fire, a river of heat consuming them both, until the fire collapsed into a thousand burning stars.

Then all was quiet and she lay still in his arms, not wanting to move away from him, savouring the languorous peace stealing over her. He kissed her softly and she snuggled deeper into his embrace, wanting to tell him of the depth of her feelings, yet not finding the words.

Later she was vaguely aware of blankets being pulled over her and she stirred, making sure he was still there.

'Don't go away,' she murmured, and he laughed.

'This is my bed,' he said, 'and I'm not going anywhere.'

*   *   *

She'd never awakened next to a man other than Matt, and seeing Jason's face on the pillow next to her, relaxed in sleep, she felt a sudden wave of guilt. It was absurd, it was utterly absurd. She knew that, yet she couldn't help the feeling.

Early morning light crept through the flowered curtains. She got up quietly, shivering in the cool morning air, and dressed quickly. She left the room without making a sound, and sat hunched in a chair outside the room watching the mist swirl around the mountain peaks.

It wasn't much later when she heard the door open and Jason came out, dressed in jeans and a sweater. He touched her hair as he passed her, sitting down in the other chair.

'Good morning.'

'Good morning.' Seeing the warmth in his eyes, she looked away, not knowing why she felt embarrassed. It was just as absurd as feeling guilty.

'Rae? Look at me.'

She met his eyes, and again she had the uneasy feeling that he could read her thoughts.

'Rae? Are you sorry?'

She shook her head. 'No.'

No, she wasn't sorry. Certainly she had known what she was doing last night. There were other, more complicated emotions. She wondered about his feelings, her own. She wondered about their motivation.

'It's all right, you know,' he said quietly. 'It's all right for us to give each other a little happiness, isn't it?'

'Yes.' She straightened in her chair, looking right at him. 'I feel guilty, can you believe that? It's ridiculous.'

'You feel as though you've been unfaithful to your husband.'

She sighed. 'That's ridiculous.'

'Not ridiculous. Perfectly natural. It's all right to feel that way; don't worry about it.'

She was surprised at his reaction and then she realised that he too had probably felt those same emotions.

'It's not you,' she said softly, her voice unsteady. 'You know that.'

'Yes, I know that.'

She shivered and pulled her jacket closer around her. Her toes were frozen. Jason came to his feet and reached for her hand. 'It's cold out here,' he said, pulling her up out of the chair. 'Let's see if we can find us a cup of *kopi*.'

Later that day they drove back to the damp heat of Semarang, leaving the cool mountain air behind.

Jason dropped Rae off at the house, and carried her small suitcase in for her, which was totally unnecessary, but an excuse to get out of view of the two girls in the back seat of the car. He held her tight for a moment and kissed her hard. 'I'll see you,' he said.

But she didn't see him again until Friday night at the Moermans' to celebrate Joost's birthday. It had seemed an endless week, with only a few glimpses of him as he dropped Anouk off at school. Problems at the job had kept him busy till all hours and he looked tired. His eyes lit up when he saw her sitting on the Moermans' large veranda and she felt the familiar stirrings in her blood at the look in his blue eyes.

'Sorry,' he said, sitting down in a chair next to her. 'I'd hoped we could go out to dinner yesterday, but at the last minute——'

She touched his hand. 'I know, it's all right.'

He gave a rueful little smile. 'It's not all right with me. I wanted to be with you.'

Coffee was poured and the birthday cake shown around to be admired. Rae had outdone herself with a rum-frosting design of terraced rice paddies and streams of water. Joost was an irrigation engineer. How a Dutchman got into irrigation wasn't quite clear to Rae. The Dutch, she'd heard, had more water than they knew what to do with and were forever pumping it out rather than into the fields.

But the cake was a great success, as was the rest of the party.

'I'm glad Anouk is doing better with her English,' Hillie said to Rae as they were in the kitchen asking the *pembantu* for more coffee. 'I'm glad you and Jason are doing better, too.' Hillie gave Rae a funny little smile and Rae wondered if Anouk had spent the night in the Moermans' Sarangan hotel room for reasons other than the kids' enjoyment. She made a face at Hillie.

'I don't kiss and tell.'

'As long as you keep kissing, I don't care. You both deserve a good dose of happiness.'

'Yes, Mother.'

Hillie rolled her eyes and walked out of the kitchen with a tray of coffee.

Happiness is good, Kate would say. As long as you realise it's just an illusion. Don't get hooked on it. It doesn't pay.

Shut up, Kate, Rae said mentally, and followed Hillie back outside.

'Anouk's birthday is next Saturday,' Jason told Rae as he drove her home after Joost's birthday had been thoroughly celebrated. 'Would you mind making her a cake?'

'Does she want me to?' Anouk was painfully polite to her, doing her work and speaking English when required, but not a word more.

'She does, but she won't ask. She seems to be harbouring some very conflicting feelings about you.'

His voice held humour. 'If she'd give herself permission, she'd like you more than a little.'

Rae felt a rush of joy. 'You think so?'

'Oh, absolutely.'

'I'll be happy to make her a cake,' she said.

'Hold the rum.'

She laughed. 'There's vanilla, chocolate, banana, coconut, lemon, orange. What would she like?'

'Anything, as long as it's sweet.' He drove through the gates and up the drive.

Rae took his hand and entwined her fingers with his. 'Would you like to come in?'

A slow smile curved his mouth. 'Yes, I would.' He leaned over to the back seat and picked up a beautifully wrapped package. 'I have something for you.'

She felt a warm glow of delight. 'Oh, thank you!' She took the package from him and he went around to open the door for her.

Inside the house everything was dark and quiet. Nicky and David were spending the weekend with friends in Solo and the house seemed twice as large and strangely empty without them.

She poured him a Scotch on the rocks, and a glass of vermouth and soda for herself. 'May I open my present now?'

He grinned. 'Please, by all means.'

It was a luxurious box of Swiss bonbons. She gave a rapturous sigh as she eyed the array of beautifully crafted chocolates. 'Forget the drink. I'll just have this.'

'Not all of them at once, I hope.' His voice held humour.

'Where did you get these? Not in Semarang, I'm sure.'

'In Jakarta. I was there on Wednesday, just for the day.'

'This is wonderful.' She put her arms around his

neck. 'Thank you.' She kissed him quickly, then drew back, but he didn't let go of her.

He smiled into her eyes. 'You're welcome,' he said softly. Then he drew her closer and kissed her. No innocent kiss, this, and her heart made somersaults in her chest.

She drew away breathlessly and leaned her head against his shoulder. Her body trembled with sweet excitement. 'Jason,' she murmured, 'please stay with me tonight.'

His arms tightened around her in answer and his kiss was long and deep and full of fire.

In her bedroom they undressed each other with eager, trembling fingers and fell on to the bed, kissing breathlessly. His hands and mouth roamed all over her and she thought she would go mad with the hunger surging through her. There was a stormy wildness in her and she responded to his caresses with primitive abandon.

She delighted in the feel and taste of his body, the heated skin against her lips, the movement of his muscles under her exploring hands.

'Rae,' he murmured, and she was stunned by the desire vibrating in his voice. 'You feel so good,' he breathed, 'so good, so good.' His lips caressed her breasts. 'I want you so much.'

It was an urgent loving, rich and full and exciting, and afterwards as she lay in his arms, happy and sated, she knew that this was where she wanted to be.

They lay drowsily on the bed and Jason gently stroked her hair, giving her soft, warm little kisses on her cheek and throat.

'I'm hungry,' she whispered after a while. 'For chocolate.'

His laugh was low and amused. 'You didn't have any yet.'

'I'll go and get them.' She slipped out of bed,

wrapped a sarong around her, and went in search of the box of bonbons.

They sat up in bed, eating chocolates, making careful selections, rating each one on a scale of one to ten. They gave each other chocolatey kisses and Rae felt utterly silly and deliciously happy and wanted the night never to end.

In the morning he woke her with soft kisses and tender touches and they made love again, drowsily and languorously, and she moaned her protest when afterwards he slipped out of her arms and out of bed.

'It's still dark.'

'I've got to go. Rini is sleeping at the house, but I don't want Anouk to think I've deserted her.'

Rini was the young girl who cleaned the house and took care of Anouk when Jason wasn't at home, but apparently he was not in the habit of staying out overnight unless he was on a trip. Rae sighed into the pillow.

Jason went into the bathroom and she heard the tap running. 'Do you mind if I use your towel?' he called.

'No, go ahead.' She was too lazy to get out of bed and get him one of his own. She smiled into the semi-darkness of the room. A man in her bed, a man in her bathroom using her towel. It was good. It felt good to be so close, so comfortable with a man, with Jason. It was wonderful to feel the delirious delight in his arms, to share the loving.

He came back into the room, naked, and she watched him as he pulled on his clothes, feeling desire curl inside her again.

He bent down and kissed her forehead. 'Go back to sleep,' he said, and quietly left the room.

On Friday afternoon Rae baked Anouk's birthday cake, spending the next morning decorating it. She'd decided on white frosting with pale pink roses for decoration, hoping Anouk would like it better than a clown's face or similar child's design. She spent hours making the roses, putting a ridiculous effort into making them especially beautiful. The cake's glory wouldn't last long—twelve little heathens would destroy it in two minutes flat. Well, that was the way it was with cakes.

The party would start at three, and she carried the cake carefully up the hill at one. Jason's car was gone, but she went into the kitchen and found Rini and Sauda mixing up pitchers of drinks.

'*Selamat siang*,' she greeted them. 'Anouk *ada*?' she asked, and Rini nodded and went in search of Anouk. The girl practically flew into the kitchen a moment later, eyes bright with expectation.

'Rini says you have something for me,' she said breathlessly, staring transfixed at the covered cake.

Rae laughed. 'Happy birthday, Anouk. I made you a cake.' She lifted the cover off and watched Anouk's face for a reaction. The grey eyes widened as she took in the delicate pink roses, the tiny buds, the soft green leaves. Her face reddened and for a moment she stood perfectly still. Then tears flooded her eyes. She gave Rae a stricken look, and with a sob ran from the kitchen, red curls flying.

Rae looked at Sauda in consternation. The woman's eyes were wide with amazement and she slowly shook her head. 'I don't understand,' she said. 'It's a beautiful cake.'

Rae had been prepared for a negative reaction, but not one like this. She wasn't sure if Anouk was ready to accept a gift from her. She wouldn't have been surprised if she'd shrugged at the cake and said she didn't like it, or something else to offend her. But not this, not these tears.

Without thinking, she leaped up the stairs to look

for Anouk, passing Rini on the landing looking con-
fused. Rae heard the crying coming from one of the
bedrooms, the room that had once been her sewing-
room. The door wasn't quite closed and she quietly
pushed it open and went in.

Anouk lay sprawled on top of the bedcover, her face
in the pillow. Her body shook with her sobs. Rae sat
down on the bed and put her hand gently on Anouk's
head. She didn't know if she was doing the right thing,
if Anouk wanted her here at all, but she simply couldn't
leave her here without her father to comfort her.

'Anouk,' she said softly. 'I'm so sorry you're
unhappy.' Under her hand she felt Anouk's sobs
subside. 'I wanted to surprise you,' she went on carefully. 'I didn't mean to make you unhappy. Is something wrong with the cake? It's all right, you can tell
me. I won't be upset.'

Anouk turned her face and looked at Rae, wide-
eyed. She sat up and wiped her face. 'Oh, no,' she
whispered 'There's nothing wrong with the cake.' She
bit her lip as if to control her crying. 'It's so beautiful.
It's the beautifullest cake I have seen in my whole life.'
Fresh tears filled her eyes. 'Oh, Mrs Smith, I'm so bad.
I'm so terrible bad.'

Rae stared at her, then put her arms around her and
held her close. There was no resistance. Anouk curled
up in her arms and cried.

'Anouk, I don't know what you're talking about,'
she said gently. 'You are not bad. What makes you
think you are bad?'

'You. . .you are so nice to me. You are always nice
to me. And I am so bad. I am so mean to you all the
time. I tell everybody you are ugly and. . .and a mean
witch, and it's not true. I am mean and you are nice.
You made a beautiful cake for me and. . .and. . .'
Another storm of weeping overtook her and Rae could
do nothing but hold her close until she finally calmed

down. She felt a pity so deep and painful, it brought tears to her own eyes.

'You're not bad, Anouk,' she said, stroking the curly hair. 'You were unhappy and you were hurting inside. It's a terrible thing to hurt inside and it makes us do things sometimes that we don't really want to do.'

'Oh, Mrs Smith, I'm so sorry. I'm so terrible sorry.'

'It's all right.' Rae lifted the tear-streaked face to look at her. 'I'm not angry. I never was angry, only worried.'

Grey eyes widened. 'You were worried about me?'

'Of course I was. I knew something was wrong. I knew you were feeling sad inside and unhappy, and I wanted to help.'

Anouk bit her trembling lip. 'I can learn English,' she said. 'I can learn a hundred words if I want to.'

Rae laughed. 'You already know more than a hundred words. I'll bet you know more than a thousand words.'

'Really?'

Rae nodded. 'Really. You're doing very well.'

Anouk let out a shuddering breath. 'I'm not going to be mean to you any more,' she declared, her mind made up.

'We'll be friends. Would you like that?'

The girl nodded solemnly. 'Yes. But I don't know what to do.'

'About what?'

'About the cake.'

Rae gently tugged at one of the red pigtails. 'You're going to eat it.'

'I don't want to.' The familiar defiance shone in her eyes and Rae suppressed a smile.

'You'll have to. All your friends are coming and they want to have a piece.'

'But it's my cake! And it's so beautiful.'

'But it's only a cake. You can't keep it.'

Anouk gave a sigh of resignation. 'I know.'

'But your father can take a picture of it and then you can always remember it.'

Anouk nodded. 'He went to the shop to buy film. He's going to take lots of pictures.'

'Good. But you'd better wash your face first.' Rae hugged her and kissed her cheek. 'Happy birthday, Anouk.'

Every afternoon, or almost every afternoon, it rained. Around four the sky would darken, the trees would begin to sway in the wind, and then suddenly the heavens would break open and rain would come pouring down in a tropical deluge that was usually over in a short time. The sky cleared, the air smelled fresh, the vegetation was clean and green.

Rae loved the rain, a break from the unrelenting heat and sunshine. Sometimes the electricity would go off and they would be without it for several hours. She would sit with Nicky and David on the veranda with candles and drinks, and smell the pungent scents of damp soil and wet vegetation. Everything was green and blooming, vines and bushes springing alive and growing rampantly. The grass lost its dry, dull colour and looked fresh and green. The flamboyant trees bloomed a fiery red, cheering the streets and gardens with their vivid flowers.

It was rambutan season and Jason brought her a bag full of the red prickly husks clustered like grapes on the stalks. Inside the husks were the soft, sweet fruits, silvery-white and slippery with large light seeds. The size of giant grapes, they easily popped into the mouth, and Rae and Jason sat on Rae's tiny veranda feeding them to each other as the tiny birds chirped in the rattan cage and the scent of flowers drifted around them on the breeze.

Happiness coloured Rae's days. Looking into the

mirror, she was amazed by the change in her face, the
light in her eyes. She was blooming like the grass and
the flowers, and the image made her smile.

If only it could last. If only it could be real and true.
She had lost once; she didn't want to lose again.

Please, she prayed, make this be real.

The man wore cowboy boots and a stetson and stood
out in the crowd in a big way. His craggy, sunburned
face positively lit up when he saw Jason, and he strode
up to him with a big grin on his face.

Rae watched him approach. It was the monthly
Sunday afternoon dinner put on by the SICO, this time
cooked and organised by the Indians in the community.
Lamb curry, chicken curry, vegetable curry. A dozen
different chutneys and condiments. Heaped bowls of
rice. Large tables were set out on the lawn around the
school house and people were eating and talking.
Children ran amok, climbing trees and swinging on the
swings.

Sometimes there were guests—visiting parents or
friends or colleagues from the head office. Whatever
category this man belonged to, the stranger approaching them was a colourful one.

The cowboy slapped Jason on the shoulder.

'Steel, ole boy, ah'll be damned!' he roared.
'Thought you'd be stuck forever in that waterlogged
frog country of Holland! Glad to see you came to your
senses. Now tell me. . .'

A white light exploded in Rae's head, cold fire froze
her blood. All she heard was the one word, *Steel*,
reverberating through her head. Steel, Steel, Steel. A
name as cold as ice. Had she heard right? Was this
some horrible nightmare? She glanced around. Everything looked as it had a few minutes ago. The grass
was so green that it hurt her eyes. The palms swayed
regally in the breeze. People were everywhere, eating

curry, talking. Yet nothing was real any more. It seemed as if she were seeing everything from far away, as if she weren't really there, but far above it all where the air was thin and frigid.

And Jason no longer seemed real as he stood there talking to the cowboy. Then she felt his arm around her shoulder and it was as heavy as a bar of steel.

'Let me introduce you——' he began, then stopped as he saw her face. 'Rae?'

Was this the man who had ruined Matt's life? She stared at Jason in frozen horror, wanting to run from him, from the truth that chilled her bones. She turned, her legs suddenly finding strength. 'I've got to go,' she mumbled, and ran, she wasn't sure where, just away. She went into the school house, opening and closing doors, blindly looking for a place, any place to hide. She wanted to be swallowed by a silent darkness where there were no colours to hurt her eyes, no words to freeze her soul.

Somewhere in a dark, windowless room, she sank to the floor and hugged herself hard, moaning as she controlled the terrible urge to scream and kick and cry.

CHAPTER SEVEN

STEEL, Steel, Steel, Rae's brain echoed.

Jason was Steel. How many other men were called Steel? Men with connections to Indonesia?

No, no. It couldn't be true. She was only dreaming this. It was some horrible mistake. She was in bed, at home, and soon she would wake up and find it was nothing but a nightmare. She would hear the tiny birds outside, the muezzin calling the devout to the temple, the roosters crowing. Slowly she opened her eyes.

She stared around the windowless room. The dusty grey light that filtered in through the crack under the door gave away only shadowy shapes and forms. It was the storage-room that had been transformed into a simple lab. She could make out the microscope on the shelf and some other equipment next to it, the vague blurs of pictures on the wall.

Steel. She shivered convulsively. No, it couldn't be true. Not Jason with his blue eyes, his gentle fingers. Not the man who warmed her with his kisses and caresses. Not the man who made love to her and made her blood sing.

Jason worked for Consultants International, not for Global Development Aid, the company for which Steel worked. Where had Jason been three years ago? Could it be that he had been with GDA at that time?

She rubbed her arms. They felt clammy and cold.

Matt. The memories came rushing back and her heart contracted with pain. Matt had wanted so very much to be overseas again. His father had been a career diplomat and Matt had spent his childhood living abroad. After ten years of college, graduate school and

117

teaching in New York, Matt had been ready to take on the world under his own power. He had found the job in Indonesia and they'd been ecstatic.

Rae, who had never been overseas before, had had reservations, yet she had been stirred up by all Matt's stories of his childhood years in Thailand and Kenya and Argentina. Of course she had gone, and she had never been sorry.

They'd been so happy in the house on the hill with the overhead fans and the veranda that caught the breeze from the ocean and the bougainvillaea drooping over the wall surrounding the compound.

It seemed hard to remember, suddenly. It was Jason who lived in the house now, and Anouk. She pushed back the image of Jason. But all she saw was his smiling mouth and the blue eyes full of love.

Steel. It was what the stranger had called him. And a man named Steel had ruined Matt's career, his life. She shivered. She was so cold, so cold, the knowledge like a rock of ice in the very centre of her body.

She didn't know how long she sat there in the dark room. Memories took over and she wasn't aware of time or place.

It had been fascinating to live in this exotic foreign place, to see how other people lived and worked and loved. 'See,' Matt had said several times, 'I knew you would like it.'

She had even found herself a teaching job at the Semarang International School, a tiny school with a dozen children from England, Germany, Japan, India, the US and several other countries.

They'd lived in Semarang for less than a year before Steel had forced Matt out, buying out his part of the contract. The Industrial Park Development Project was large and ambitious and both governments—the American and Indonesian—were watching with hawk eyes. To have been awarded even such a small contract of this prestigious project had been a dream come true for restless, adventurous Matt, who had been looking for a way to go overseas for years.

After their return to the States, Matt had never been the same. He had not wanted to go back to his old teaching job at the university, even though he had been an excellent instructor who was popular with his students. There had been no choice.

The months that followed their return had been miserable. Rae hadn't known how to make him happy, how to keep him from drinking too much. The tragedy had happened one night at a large beach party, several days after they'd heard a report on the IPD project in Indonesia. Everything had been going better than expected, thanks to Steel, who had moved temporarily to Jakarta to take charge and force changes. After dark, Matt, with too many drinks in his system, had gone swimming and drowned. Even to that day, Rae wondered if he had gone out on purpose or just out of recklessness.

'Oh, Matt,' she whispered, tears running down her cheeks, 'why did you do it? Why did you leave me?'

She started when a light suddenly flooded the room.

'Rae! Good God, I've looked all over for you!'

Jason hovered over her, staring down at her as she sat hunched on the floor. Silence quivered around them.

'Go away,' she said, almost choking on the words.

'Rae, what's wrong?' There was concern in his voice, but she wanted none of it, none of him.

'Just go away.' She wiped at her face, which was wet with tears. She hugged her knees tighter to her chest and averted her face.

'I'm not going away.' His voice was calm and determined. 'Why are you sitting on the floor, for God's sake? What's going on?'

'Nothing! Just leave me alone!'

He sat down on his haunches in front of her, reaching out as if to touch her, but she moved away from his hands, further into the corner. 'You're crying,' he said. 'That's not nothing. Did I say something? Did I do something?'

She forced down a hysterical giggle. You ruined my life, that's what you did, she wanted to say, but she swallowed the bitter words. Yet she had to say something, find some way to get rid of him, but she couldn't think of what.

'Rae? Are you going to tell me?'

'Tell you what? There's nothing to tell.' Tears filled her eyes again. 'I want to go home. I feel sick. I just want to be alone.' She couldn't help the tears, the cold misery that made her body shake.

He drew her up off the floor and held her against him. 'Tell me,' he ordered.

She struggled wildly. 'Leave me alone!' she sobbed. 'I don't want you touching me!'

Voices, laughter. People entered the hallway. Rae tore herself away and ran out of the door, back outside where the sun drenched the world in a glaring white light. Jason followed her. He gripped her arm. 'I'll take you home.'

'No! I'll go by myself.'

'No, you won't.' It was said with finality. He took her arm and marched her over to the car and deposited her into the passenger's seat. She sat hunched in the seat, trying to still the crying, shivering despite the heat. She didn't even know what she was crying for any more—Matt, the loss of a dream, Jason, who wasn't the man she'd thought he was, the utter disillusionment of it all. She hated him; she hated him for what he had done to her, what he was doing now.

They drove to the house in silence. Rae got out before Jason had a chance to open the door for her.

The back door was open and she walked in, knowing

Jason would follow her whether she wanted him to or not. She didn't know what to do any more. She didn't care. She felt exhausted and defeated, and all she wanted now was the silence of her room and the oblivion of sleep.

She took a deep breath and turned to face him. 'Thank you for bringing me home. I'll take some aspirin and go to bed.'

He wasn't fooled for a minute. 'Rae,' he said quietly, 'please talk to me.'

She shook her head. 'No, I can't.' She closed her eyes briefly. 'I just need to be alone now.'

There was a silence, and she was aware of his eyes searching her face, but she didn't look at him. She didn't want to see his face, his eyes. She didn't want to remember his face when he had held her, had made love to her. She stared blindly at the floor.

'All right,' he said at last, 'I'll leave.'

But I'll be back, was the unspoken message, and she didn't miss it.

She couldn't sleep that night. Maybe I heard wrong, she kept thinking. Maybe it was all a mistake. Jason could not be the man she had pictured as Steel, the cruel, power-hungry man. Jason wasn't like that.

But what if he was? What if she had been wrong about him all along? What if he was hiding that darker side of him from her? There were stories of women married to men for years before they found out their true natures. Treachery, deceit, unfaithfulness, all craftily obscured.

Now she herself had fallen in love with a man she didn't know.

Jason wasn't a man to give up easily, and Rae wasn't surprised when she saw him coming down the road the next afternoon as she sat on her veranda trying to read. It was Monday, and in order to avoid Jason she'd decided not to go to the Hash run; apparently he'd had the same idea. He came striding purposefully towards the house and her pulse quickened. He came around to the back and towards her veranda, leaping easily up the few steps.

'Hello, Rae,' he said, blue eyes looking at her searchingly.

Her body tensed and it took an effort to return the greeting.

He leaned against the wall, his eyes still fixed on her face. 'I want to talk about what happened yesterday,' he said without preamble. 'I have to know. I'm worried and I want to know what it is that upset you so.' His voice was quietly determined, and she knew he would not leave this time until she had told him what he had come to find out.

'I'm worried about you, Rae,' he said softly.

Her heart froze. She didn't want to be taken in by his gentleness. She bit her lip, hard. 'That cowboy called you Steel last night. Did I hear that right?'

He frowned. 'Yes. What does that have to do with anything?'

'Where did you get that name?' she asked, ignoring his question.

He shrugged. 'Just a nickname I picked up a few years ago.'

'Did you ever work for Global Development Aid?'

'I managed the Asia division.'

Her heart sank. It was true. This wasn't all a nightmare. 'You had a project here in Indonesia, didn't you? The Industrial Park Development Project, right?'

'Yes.' He frowned. 'Rae, what is all this? What are you talking about?'

'Does the name Matt Smith mean anything to you?'

'Matt Smith? I know a Richard Smith.'

'*Matthew* Smith!' He didn't remember Matt. He didn't even remember! Fury raced through her.

'*Matthew* Smith!' she repeated. 'The man you bought out of the project three years ago! Because you wanted it all for yourself. You wanted to run the whole show, and Matt was in your way!'

He stared at her, then his face paled. 'Matthew Smith,' he said slowly. 'Your husband.'

'Yes! My husband. I'm so glad you've managed to remember now,' she said caustically. 'It's a lot harder for me to forget!'

'Oh, my God,' he muttered. 'I'm sorry.'

'I'll bet you are!'

She stared at him through her tears, despair mingling with her anger. She wiped at her eyes and she saw him look at her, silent and frowning.

'I don't understand why you're so upset,' he said. 'We bought him out fairly.'

'You *forced* him out! You gave him no choice!'

'Rae——'

'Isn't it true? Just tell me that! Isn't it true that you gave him no choice?'

The silence screamed in her ears, then he sighed. 'It's true,' he said then.

She could feel the cold radiating all through her, numbing her toes, her fingers. 'That's all I wanted to know.' She straightened her shoulders. 'I'm sorry I didn't know who you were earlier, but I know now.'

There was a terrible silence.

'What is it that you know?'

She could see the restraint in him, hear the forced calm of his voice. She didn't care.

'You're self-serving and greedy. You wanted all the credit for the IPD project! It was big and important and you wanted your name on it! You had to get rid of Matt because he was in your way. And you did! Oh, you did it with money, probably to salve your conscience—not that I think you have one.' She was saying things she would never have dreamed of saying to anybody, the words dropping like icicles from her tongue. She didn't know what was happening to her. Some terrible pain and anger possessed her and there was nothing to hold back the flow of words, no inner restraint, no self-control. It was all gone. All she saw was this man who was responsible for what had happened to Matt.

'You ruined my husband's life. You ruined mine.'

She saw the anger flare in his eyes, the steely chin as he clamped his jaws hard together. Without another word he turned and walked down the veranda steps into the garden.

She sank down in a chair, covered her face with her hands as a storm of weeping overwhelmed her. 'I loved him, don't you understand? I loved him!'

Nicky found her moments later, her green eyes wide with concern.

'Oh, my God, Rae, what happened? What did Jason do?' She sat down next to Rae and put an arm around her shoulder.

Rae pressed her palms against her eyes. Brilliant colours exploded in her brain. 'I hate him,' she said fiercely. 'I hate him!'

'Why? What did he do?'

'I didn't know who he was! I was so stupid. I should never have fallen for him!' She almost choked on the words. 'He's just another egomaniac grasping for power and prestige, and he doesn't care who gets in the way, or who gets hurt!'

'Rae, what in heaven's name are you talking about?'

'Jason is the one who got rid of Matt! He's the one who bought him out and forced him to leave.'

Nicky paled. 'Oh, my God.' She bit her lip, looking at Rae with painful surprise. 'How do you know?'

Rae told her, the words and sentences dropping in short, bitter syllables from her mouth.

'There's got to be some explanation,' Nicky said. 'Maybe something we don't know about.'

'All I know is that Matt worked twelve hours a day! All he wanted was to do the job and do it well. He brought work home all the time. He was dedicated and enthusiastic and he wanted the project to succeed.'

'And yet Jason got rid of him.'

'Right. You know how it happened. You were there.'

Nicky groaned. 'It was awful. Matt was so depressed.' She was silent, then she let out a deep sigh. 'God, Rae, I don't know what to think. I like Jason. I can't imagine him playing power games.'

'You never know, do you?' The bitterness in Rae's voice was ill-concealed. She thought of Kate saying that sooner or later men would desert you or cheat on you or prove not to be worth holding on to. Well, she had been right.

'Did you ask him?' Nicky asked.

'Did I ask him what?'

'About what happened.'

'He didn't deny anything. When I asked him if he had forced Matt out he said yes.'

'I can't understand why he would do that. Maybe there's something we don't understand.'

'Like what?' Rae heard the hostility in her voice. 'Do you think Matt was dishonest, corrupt, swindled money?'

'Of course I don't.' Nicky sighed again. 'I'm sorry, Rae, I'm just trying to figure it out. I'm not insinuating anything.'

Rae bit her lip, trying to control her tears. 'I'm sorry. I don't mean to take my frustrations out on you.'

Nicky gave a funny half smile and squeezed Rae's hand. 'Hey, what are friends for?'

* * *

Rae didn't know how she made it through the next few weeks. It was painful to see Jason. She avoided him whenever she could, but in a small community such as theirs there was no hiding.

On the up side, there was Anouk, whose attitude had turned around a hundred and eighty degrees.

'My grandfather and grandmother are coming here,' she announced one day, her small face alight with joy. 'Yesterday evening we telephoned them. They come to eat and sleep in our house.'

'That's wonderful, Anouk,' Rae smiled. 'It must make you very happy. I never had any grandparents.'

Anouk's eyes widened. 'Are they dead?'

Rae nodded. 'Three of them. One of my grandfathers went away and they don't know where he is.'

'That's terrible. Does everybody worry about him?'

'I don't think so. He was not a good man.'

'Oh.' She frowned. 'I don't think my grandfather will go away.'

Rae smiled. 'I don't think so, either.'

'He's a very, very good man. Only he smokes cigars and they smell.' She screwed up her face. 'Yuk.'

Rae laughed. 'Oh, well, not even grandfathers can be perfect. I guess that's the way it is.'

'Well, I'm sorry you don't have grandparents. It's nice to have them.' Anouk grinned. 'They give you presents and they take you to the. . .the. . .' She frowned, searching for a word. 'Animal garden,' she said then. 'I know that's not the right word, but I can't remember.'

'Zoo,' Rae supplied.

'Oh, yes! Zoo, zoo, zoo,' she sang as she danced away, her pigtails swinging.

Rae stared after her, joy warming her. It was wonderful to have a conversation with Anouk without hostility or mistrust. It was something to be happy about.

After dinner that night she was sitting in her room, writing a letter, when someone knocked on her door.

'Come in,' she said automatically, looking up from her writing.

Jason entered the room. 'Hello, Rae,' he said quietly, and a shock of emotion rippled through her.

'I thought it was Nicky.'

'She told me to come and find you; she was on the phone.'

Rae's heart was beating erratically. She didn't want him here in her room. It was too small and intimate a space. She didn't want all those confusing, painful feelings he called up in her.

All she wanted was to forget whatever there had been between them. But forgetting was not so easy, she knew that.

After Matt's death so many things had reminded her of him: the colour of a towel, the shape of someone else's hands, the smell of bacon. For months she'd been unable to eat bacon.

Now everything made her think of Jason: chocolate, stars on a clear night, the taste of rambutan fruit.

There was no way to avoid him in this small town. If only she could just forget. . .if only she didn't feel the pain and anger. But it was there, all the time, no matter how hard she tried not to feel it.

He closed the door behind him. 'I would like to talk to you, Rae.'

'There's nothing to talk about.'

He held her gaze. 'I miss you.'

She felt tears crowding behind her eyes. 'Well, *I* miss my husband!'

His face paled. She saw the pain in his eyes and she felt herself grow cold and hard inside. She didn't want him to have any power over her. She didn't want to feel anything when it came to Jason Grant. She owed it to Matt, to herself.

'I loved my husband,' she said. 'He was a wonderful man. He was smart and funny and I loved him.' Her voice broke. 'And I lost him. It wouldn't have happened if he hadn't had to go back home. I would still be married to him.' Tears were rolling down her cheeks. All she could see was Jason's face, pale and desolate, and somehow Matt's face wasn't there in her mind. She couldn't call it up. It was gone, gone. 'I loved him,' she cried, helpless now to keep herself under control, wanting more than anything to see Matt's face to help her, give her courage. 'I loved him.'

'I know,' he said quietly. 'I know you loved him, but you cannot blame me for his death.'

'Why not? You made him go back home!'

He was silent.

'Didn't you?'

'Yes, I did.'

'And what did he do? Did he not work hard enough? Did he accept bribes? Did he do something fraudulent? Did he embezzle money?'

'No, Rae, no.' He closed his eyes. 'He would have been fired, straight and simple.'

'Then why did you buy him out? Tell me that?'

'It was in the best interest of the project.'

'The project! I'm sick and tired of hearing about your beloved project! Matt spent every waking hour working on that project. To you the damned project was more important than the people working for it! Matt wasn't the only one to go, was he? Oh, I heard the stories! You weren't called Steel for nothing, now, were you?'

'All this happened years ago, Rae. It has nothing to do with you and me.'

'How dare you say that? It has everything to do with you and me!'

'Rae, please listen to me.' He came a little closer, but she backed away from him.

'Don't touch me! Just leave me alone!' She opened the door and left the room, leaving him standing there. It was the bleakness in his eyes that followed her down the hallway into the main part of the house. She steeled herself against it. How could she possibly feel anything for him now, after she knew what he had done to Matt?

Nicky and David were sitting on the veranda, reading.

'Sit down,' Nicky said. 'David was just getting us a drink. Do you want something?'

'Anything strong,' she said, her voice quavering. She twisted her hands together to keep them from shaking, and sat down.

'Did Jason go?'

'I don't know, I just left him.' She bit her lip, hard. 'And please, don't send him to my room again. I don't want to see him.'

She had no control over her dreams. And it was Jason haunting her nights—Jason kissing her, Jason making love to her. There was the silent lake and the stars above it, and Jason, always Jason. He came to her in the night, in her dreams, telling her he loved her. Once she awoke crying.

She caught glimpses of him as he dropped Anouk off at school, but he did not attempt to speak to her again. School closed for the month of December. A number of people left town, spending the holidays in Bali or going on home-leave to the States or Europe. Nicky and David were planning a Christmas dinner for some of the ones who stayed behind.

'I'll bake,' Rae said, 'but I'm not good with turkey.'

Kevin dropped by one evening saying he was going to spend a week in Singapore for interviews. His contract was up in six months and he was being head-hunted in a serious way by one of the biggest engineering companies in the East.

'Come with me,' he invited. 'I've got a two-room suite at the Jasmine, all paid for. You can do your Christmas shopping in the day and we can go out at night.'

It was a tempting offer, and not something she could possibly have afforded on her own with the price of hotel rooms way out of her range.

'Why don't you?' said Nicky. 'You've got time now, and a free room at the Jasmine is excuse enough. We stayed there a couple of nights last year. It's sinfully luxurious. You'll love Singapore. It's very clean and efficient and the shopping is incredible.' She grinned. 'And while you're there, I'd like you to pick up a couple of things for me.'

Singapore. Such an exotic name! She'd love to find out what the place was like. A little diversion would be wonderful. And, with Kevin there, the evenings would be fun.

'Are you sure you want me there with you?'

'What else am I going to do at night? Sit in my hotel room? Or hunt for women in a bar?'

She grinned. 'That's one idea. Isn't that what all men do when they go on business trips?'

'Not this one. I'm not that desperate.'

'He's a prince,' Nicky said to Rae. 'I wonder why he hasn't been snatched up yet.'

'Go ahead,' he said, 'make fun of me. What do you know of my nightly torments, all alone in that big house that cries out for a woman's touch, the sounds of children playing——'

Nicky rolled her eyes. 'David, get the man another beer, will you?'

Just being away from Semarang lifted some of the depression she'd felt lately. Sitting in the plane, Rae could pretend that she was leaving behind everything that had happened. She would not think about Jason, she promised herself. She was simply going to enjoy a week in Singapore.

A hotel limousine picked them up at Changi Airport, the driver in starched whites. Rae surveyed the scenery as the car cruised smoothly through the wide streets. Everything was clean and orderly and modern, a different world only an hour and a half away from Jakarta. In many ways it seemed like a western city with oriental people, women in the latest fashions, men in well-cut business suits. No beggars on the streets, no rickety trucks overloaded with cabbages, no unhelmeted motorcycle riders.

Even from the outside it was easy to see that the Jasmine Hotel was the ultimate in luxury. A smiling doorman in immaculate uniform opened the limousine door and ushered them into the spacious lobby with its marble floor, huge palms, and crystal chandeliers. Rae sucked in her breath with awe as she glanced around, taking in the exquisite Chinese rugs, the comfortable chairs grouped around low tables, with exotic flower arrangements offering a serene mix of western comfort and oriental elegance. It was like something out of a film, something utterly and superbly beautiful.

An assistant manager accompanied them to their suite, and shortly afterwards jasmine tea was delivered to the room in a delicate Chinese pot with matching cups. The tea was accompanied by chocolate bonbons and a beautiful tray of oriental fruits.

'Who is paying for all this?' she asked Kevin, who was tearing off his tie as if it were an offending noose.

'The company.'

'But why two rooms?'

'They suggested I bring my wife and kids to see what they thought of the city. They know a man is more apt to make a move if the wife is involved and positive.'

'But you don't have a wife and children.'

'I told them that. They said to bring a companion

instead. They were not so cheap as to cancel the
reservations and get a single for me. They're a classy
outfit.'

'They must want you badly.'

'They do.' He grinned. 'I'm not so sure I want them,
but we'll see.'

She wondered if she had underrated Kevin. Kevin
with all his rough edges and his brawny attitude was
becoming quite a surprise.

She went shopping that same afternoon, feeling not
at all tired. An enormous shopping mall was attached
to the hotel, connected with a delicate-looking covered
walkway, its supports entwined with fragrant, blooming
jasmine vines. She spent several hours looking through
all the opulent luxuries, deciding she would buy herself
a dinner dress so that she would feel quite at home in
the luxurious hotel. Or maybe just to please herself.

She didn't buy one, she bought two, feeling deliciously decadent, feeling good about looking wonder-
fully feminine and elegant. She treated herself to a
facial in the hotel beauty salon, then had her hair done
as well, which included with the shampoo a marvel-
lously relaxing scalp massage. She topped it all off with
a manicure. I might as well go the whole way, she
thought, feeling sinfully pampered by the delicate
Malaysian beauty who touched her hands as if they
were precious jewels.

Kate, she thought, you should see me now.

The Malaysian girl spoke to her in a gentle, melodi-
ous voice, asking her what she thought of Singapore
and if she enjoyed the Jasmine. Rae was eager to ask
her about her life, where she lived, if she was married,
how she grew up, but the girl was so perfectly pro-
fessional that it was impossible to be so indiscreet. Rae
thought of the place she had her hair done in New
York, a very nice place indeed with competent hair-
stylists, but the conversation was often very personal—
ranging from boyfriends to birthing experiences.

She found a message from Kevin on her return to her room, asking her to be ready for dinner at eight and saying that a Mr Lee and his wife would be joining them. She was glad she had bought the dresses and had her hair done. It wasn't six yet, so she had plenty of time to get ready. She ordered a cup of *cappuccino*, which was brought only minutes later on a beautiful bamboo tray with a cloth napkin and a single pink rose.

Afterwards she had a long soak in the shiny bathtub, the water fragrant with jasmine-scented crystals, and she wondered fuzzily what it would be like to be wealthy and live in this luxury all the time. Most likely you would get used to it and think nothing of it.

She took her time dressing, smiling at her reflection in the mirror. She looked superbly elegant in the cream-and-coffee-coloured silk dress, which went perfectly with her hazel eyes and chestnut hair, as the Chinese salesgirl had suggested. She had been right. 'Not black for you,' she'd said, as Rae had longingly eyed a glamorous little black creation. 'It's too stark for your colouring.' The other dress was a delicate jade-green silk in an elegant classical style that would go to many places. Even in her extravagant mood, she could not throw all caution to the wind.

She twirled in front of the floor-to-ceiling mirror. Money could buy a lot, if not everything, and she gazed at herself in the mirror, trying hard not to think of what she wanted most in life, which was not for sale for any amount of money.

'Enjoy this while it lasts,' she said to her reflection.

At twenty past seven she heard Kevin enter his room. He came straight through to the sitting-room, where she was sitting on the sofa going through a number of slick booklets and leaflets provided by the hotel. The visitor to Singapore was told where to dine out, where to find the various attractions, what to see in terms of theatre and the arts. By the looks of it there

was no need to be bored. The citizens of the island-city
of Singapore made up an interesting mix of Malaysians,
Chinese and Indians, creating a diversity of culture,
not always entirely harmonious, but creating a rich
blend of festive events and cuisines.

She glanced up and found Kevin staring at her.
'Good lord,' he muttered. 'You look stunning.'

She smiled. 'Thank you.'

He glanced at his watch. 'I'll run through the shower
and get dressed and then we'll go.'

He appeared some twenty minutes later, dressed in
an immaculate dark suit, white shirt and dark tie,
looking strikingly handsome. She was used to seeing
him in faded jeans, tacky shorts or casual lightweight
clothes, and this metamorphosis was quite a surprise.

He grinned at her, seeing her amazement. 'Didn't
think I had it in me, did you? Well, I promised you I'd
show you the finer side of me one day.'

She laughed. 'Obviously the day has arrived. No
sheep herder, are you?'

He wrinkled his nose. 'Sheep smell,' he said. He
reached out his hand to help her up. 'Are you ready?'

They ordered drinks in the elegant cocktail lounge
where soon they were joined by Mr and Mrs Lee, one
of the Chinese vice-presidents of the firm interviewing
Kevin, and his wife.

Mr Lee and his wife seemed somewhat formal, which
was probably appropriate. However, by the time they
sat down at their table they had loosened up a little,
and when Rae asked Mrs Lee to help her select
something from the menu she turned quite enthusiastic,
whispering with a smile that the best food in Singapore,
really, was to be found in the streets at the stalls of the
food vendors.

Rae smiled back. So here I am, in one of the poshest
hotels in the world, she thought, and she tells me to go
and eat in the streets.

They ordered a variety of Chinese dishes, the selection of which she and Kevin left entirely up to the Lees.

'Well, look who's here,' Kevin said suddenly, looking past Rae's head. She turned to see and her heart gave a sickening lurch.

Jason, dressed in a dark suit, entered the dining-room accompanied by Anouk and an older couple. She felt a rush of pain, a dizzy sense of disorientation. Her heart raced as if she'd run a marathon. She took a deep breath, letting it out slowly, trying futilely to calm herself. Jason. What was Jason doing here? All day she had tried so desperately not to think of him, to enjoy this special time here away from it all, and now he was here. How *dared* he be here and disturb her peace of mind?

Anouk came rushing over. 'Mrs Smith? I didn't know you were here! Are you sleeping in this hotel, too?' Rae saw her through a haze. Her hair was put up in a sophisticated little bun at the back. She wore a white dress and tiny pearl earrings in her ears. She was so much a little lady that Rae, despite her confusion, couldn't help but smile.

'You look beautiful, Anouk.'

The girl slid her hand down the skirt of the dress. 'We just bought it this afternoon. My grandmother helped me.' She twirled around. 'I want you to meet my grandmother and grandfather. I call them *Oma* and *Opa*. I like that better.'

Rae smiled, shook hands, aware of Jason standing only feet away, looking at her. She didn't like the expression on his face. She had no idea how they had ended up here in the same hotel. It could not possibly be a coincidence, could it? There were too many luxury hotels in Singapore for this to happen coincidentally— the Mandarin, the Oriental, Raffles. Why was he here at the Jasmine?

'Today we eat here,' Anouk babbled cheerfully, 'but they have promised that tomorrow we go to McDonald's. They have everything here, did you know that? Even pizza! I saw it on TV. I like the TV here.'

'I'm glad you're having fun,' Rae said, her smile encompassing the girl and the grandparents.

Further introductions were made and, after the exchange of a few civilities, Jason manoeuvred his family away to another table.

Shaken, Rae stared at the delicate flower arrangement in the middle of the table. She felt nervous, and then suddenly deeply, painfully angry.

'Did you know Jason was staying here?' she asked Kevin, trying hard to keep her voice cool and casual. He shook his head, his glass halfway to his mouth.

'No idea. Quite a coincidence, I should say.' He seemed unconcerned.

The food arrived, beautifully served and exquisitely presented. Rae tried to concentrate on the food, the conversation, but she was painfully aware of Jason and his clan sitting not far away, but out of her view. Was she imagining his eyes on the back of her head? It made her nervous and irritable, and it took an effort to pay attention to the conversation.

Mrs Lee asked her to please call her by her given name, and would she like to have her show her the more interesting parts of the city? Have some lunch at the stalls at Rasa Singapura? She suggested that most certainly Kevin should take Rae on a harbour cruise in a Chinese junk. 'It's very romantic at sunset,' she said, smiling. 'Don't miss it.'

Rae didn't want to go on a romantic cruise with Kevin. She didn't want any more romance in her life, ever. It brought only pain.

After the meal was finished, Kevin took her up to the suite and then went back down to the nightclub for another drink with the Lees. She had declined to go with them, wanting to be alone, not to have to smile and be polite when all she could see in her mind was Jason, all she could hear was his deep voice.

She surveyed the beautifully decorated room, the big comfortable bed, thinking of that other room—small and shabby with the fire in the fireplace and the stubby white candles. All this luxury meant nothing; she was alone and the bed was big and empty. She had no one to hold on to, no one to love.

She hung her dress carefully in the wardrobe. Why had she even bought these two dresses? Just to help her forget that it was really Jason she wanted, really Jason she wanted to be with. But nothing could make her forget, no elegant hotel and exquisite meals, no beautiful dresses or romantic harbour cruises.

After her shower she wrapped herself in a large terrycloth bathrobe and sat on the bed, which had been neatly turned back. She wondered what to do now. She wasn't tired. She didn't feel like reading. She didn't want to watch television.

The knock on the outer door surprised her. She opened it to find Jason standing there, one hand leaning up against the door-jamb. His jacket had gone and he had taken off his tie and turned up the cuffs of his shirt-sleeves. He looked grim and determined. Big, frightening.

Her body went rigid, her hand gripped the doorknob until her fingers ached.

His eyes looked directly into hers. 'I want to talk to you,' he said.

CHAPTER EIGHT

JASON moved into the room without waiting for Rae's answer and closed the door firmly behind him. In the tanned face, his eyes blazed a bright blue. Her heart thumped wildly. 'I don't want to talk to you! And what do you think you're doing, barging in here at this hour of the night?'

He raked his hand through his hair in a weary gesture. Deep lines of fatigue ran beside his mouth, and she steeled herself against the emotions welling up inside.

He sighed heavily. 'Please, let's not argue.'

'Why are you here in Singapore?' she demanded. 'And how did you know I was staying at the Jasmine? Don't tell me it's coincidence!' She clutched the lapels of her robe in her hand, uneasily aware that she was wearing nothing underneath. Aware of the terrible attraction he still held over her.

He put his hands in his pockets. 'I'm here to pick up my in-laws. They could have come straight to Jakarta, but I thought we'd take in a little Christmas shopping and show them the city.' He shrugged. 'I'd planned it that way.'

'Why the Jasmine?'

His eyes held hers. 'Because you're here.' His mouth quirked as if mildly mocking himself for his folly.

At least he wasn't lying. 'And how did you know I was here?'

He shrugged impatiently. 'Oh, come on, now. Everybody knows everything in Semarang. Didn't you tell me that once? I heard somebody mentioning you going to Singapore with Kevin, so I found out.'

She gritted her teeth. 'So why are you here, then? I don't like being followed around.' She'd come here to get away from him, for a short reprieve from the tension, hoping it might just possibly give her a different perspective.

'I'm here hoping to prevent you from doing something stupid.'

Her laugh was short and low and held no amusement. 'Like what?'

'I shouldn't have to spell it out, Rae, should I?'

No, he shouldn't. He didn't like her being here with Kevin. Well, that was just too bad! She squared her shoulders and met his eyes. 'You're not my keeper. Why don't you mind your own business?' Her legs were shaking and she sank down on the edge of the bed.

'You are my business, whether you want it that way or not. I'm more sorry than you know for what happened, but I wish——'

'Well, straighten out your head and stop wishing!' She jumped back to her feet, anger washing over her with new strength. 'I don't want you! I've said it and I mean it!' Her voice shook and, to her horror, tears came to her eyes.

'I don't believe that, Rae.' His voice was so quiet, his blue eyes so calm that for a terrifying moment she feared he could see right into her very soul. She looked away, swallowing against the tears.

'Why don't you just leave me alone?' she said thickly. 'Why do you have to spoil my vacation?'

'I don't mean to spoil your vacation.'

'Then leave me alone!'

'No.' He came forward and took her shoulders, staring hard into her eyes. 'You're here with Kevin, in this hotel that you can't possibly afford. Who is paying for this room, tell me that?'

She was trembling with fury, with all sorts of conflicting emotions.

'What do you know about my finances? Nothing! Maybe my husband was smart enough to buy a huge life-insurance policy in case he would accidentally on purpose drown himself in the Atlantic.' Her voice was cold and bitter and it sounded like the voice of a stranger. She saw him flinch. Then his face hardened again and she felt his fingers grip hard into her shoulders.

'Let go of me!' she choked.

He ignored her. 'Who's paying for this room?'

'Kevin is paying for this room,' she said, wanting to hurt him, hating herself for feeling what she was feeling, this horrible mixture of need and love and hate. She couldn't love this man. She could never love the man who had ruined Matt.

And then he was kissing her, hard and desperate, and she fought against him, against her own treacherous emotions, tears rolling down her cheeks. But she was no match for his strength, and his arms held her like steely bands. She felt the heat of his body, smelled the warm, familiar scent of his skin as his mouth hungrily took hers. She could do nothing but stand there with all the longing and despair washing over her, not fighting any longer. She wanted him. She loved him. She hated him.

His mouth moved to her cheeks, her temples, her eyes, kissing her damp face. 'Oh, God,' he groaned, 'don't cry. Don't cry.'

She wrenched herself free. 'I hate you!' she sobbed. 'I hate you!' She clutched the robe tighter around her, backing away from him.

His face went ashen under his tan. 'No, you don't, Rae,' he said softly. 'Don't deny your true feelings. What we had together was special. Please let's not destroy it.'

'What we had was *nothing*! An illusion. A terrible mistake. All I want is for you to be out of my life!'

'Rae, please listen to me.' His voice was husky with emotion, his eyes dark and tormented. 'Don't do this to yourself. No matter what happened between us, don't get involved with Kevin; he's no good for you.'

'*You* are no good for me! If you knew what was good for me you wouldn't have made Matt go home!'

She saw him flinch, but the pain in his eyes gave her no satisfaction. Oh, God, she thought, I'm no good at hating. I can't stand this.

He went to the door and opened it. For a long moment he looked at her, his eyes so intense that it frightened her. It seemed as if he were ready to say something, then he changed his mind, his jaw clenched in the effort. He turned and strode out of the room without another word, closing the door quietly behind him.

She threw herself on the bed and wept.

The excitement of being on the garden island of Singapore had dulled significantly, although for small stretches of time she did forget about Jason and enjoyed the surroundings, the magnificent parks, the exotic Chinatown, the delicious food. Apparently the modern, western part of the city with its wide streets and tall office buildings was only a part of the city. Mrs Lee was a wonderful guide, showing her places she wouldn't have known to find on her own.

On their second night Kevin took her to the historic Raffles Hotel and they sat in the bar drinking Singapore Slings, which was such an utterly touristy thing to do, it made her laugh. But the white Victorian building was magnificent with its old-world charm and, later, dinner on the large covered veranda with its slowly moving fans was a culinary delight.

'Well, you know what Rudyard Kipling said,' Kevin commented.

Rae sat back in the white wrought-iron chair and shook her head. 'No, I don't, I'm afraid. I'm culturally deprived.'

'"Feed at Raffles when in Singapore,"' Kevin quoted.

Rae laughed. 'Delicately put.'

On Wednesday night the Jasmine Hotel presented a *Malam Singapura*, a dinner and a cultural show performed in the open air by the pool.

The dance and song show was exciting and exotic, the girls in opulent eastern costumes in jewelled colours sensuous and elegant. The air was balmy and fragrant with jasmine that grew luxuriantly all around the exquisite hotel garden. In the enjoyment of it all Rae forgot everything until she noticed Jason, Anouk and her grandparents at a table in the far corner. Her spirits sank to rock-bottom. I should have known they'd be here, she thought. Of course they'd be here.

At intermission, Anouk slipped through the tables and stood by Rae's chair, eyes shining.

'The girls are so beautiful, don't you think, Mrs Smith?'

'They are. Are you having a good time?'

'Oh, yes! But I don't like the food.' She wrinkled her nose. 'It tastes funny.'

'Did you go to McDonald's on Monday?'

'Yes. It looked almost the same as the one at home.'

'In Holland?'

'Yes. In the town where my *opa* and *oma* live. Sometimes we went there to eat.'

'What did you do today?'

'We went to the bird park today and Papa bought a Chinese mask for me. It's very scary! They use them for feasts. If I put it on for Sander, he scare himself dead!' Her face gleamed with delicious anticipation. 'This is a very fun place! I must go back now.'

Kevin laughed. 'She's got the devil in her eyes, that one.'

To Rae's relief, Jason did not come to their table and he did not visit her in her room. Not that she would have opened the door to him this time, she thought grimly.

The next few days she spent a lot of time browsing through small side-street shops, through Chinatown and Little India, where she looked with fascination at all the colourful items on display, the jewellery, the lovely silk saris. The air was fragrant with the scent of exotic spices and curries cooking.

A bearded, turbaned Indian with piercing black eyes wanted to tell her fortune, but she passed him by. She couldn't imagine anything very good, and she already knew the bad news.

Yet at the corner of the street she stopped and hesitated, seeing in her mind's eye the man's black eyes, wondering if just maybe he could see something good in her future. Surely there was something worth hoping for? Even if it was all in your head, a dream was worth having, wasn't it?

Once, as a teenager, she'd gone to a gypsy fortune-teller with two of her friends. It had been a snowy, foggy day between Christmas and New Year, and she remembered the damp and the fearful shivering as they'd stood in front of the paintless door of the woman's shabby apartment. She'd thought gypsies lived in trailers and stole horses.

The apartment had been very dark and smelled of boiled cabbage, and the old crone had made them wait for ten minutes before she let them in. As they'd stood on the landing, waiting, a black cat had scooted past them and they'd almost fled back down the stairs out of sheer fright.

The gypsy had worn voluminous skirts, a black shawl around her head and long dangly earrings, all of which were what Rae had expected. The woman had peered into her crystal ball and told each of them their fortunes. Rae was going to marry the man of her dreams, who was blond and blue-eyed and a great athlete. They'd be very rich and have three children and live in a big house by the sea. Dizzy with delight, she'd gone home. She had indeed been in love with a tall blond basketball player, whose father was very rich, which was almost the same. That night she'd dreamed of walking hand in hand with him along the beach, with the water lapping at their bare feet and gulls swooping overhead.

Unfortunately, Gregory had never asked her out, not even to the pictures, and some years later she'd heard that he had gone to Europe, married an impoverished Spanish *condesa* and lived in a dilapidated castle on a mountaintop overlooking vast olive groves.

But she had married the man of her dreams, eventually, though he had not been blond and blue-eyed, or particularly athletic. There had not been a house near the sea and there had been no children.

Someone bumped into her, muttering an apology, and Rae moved on, away from the turbaned Indian and his promises of good fortune. At a small stall she bought a triangular *samosa*, a pastry with a spicy meat and vegetable filling, and she sat on a rickety bench as she ate it, watching the people go by, the women dressed in saris, the children with their big, dark eyes ringed with kohl.

She ended up with quite a collection of small Christmas presents, and was pleased with herself. A wooden statuette of the monkey god for Kevin, a pair of dangling Indian earrings of silver filigree for Nicky, a small rose-quartz figurine of a Chinese goddess for Hillie. She'd bought a small lacquer box for Anouk in

Chinatown, thinking of the tiny earrings she'd seen her wear in the hotel restaurant.

On their last night in Singapore, Kevin insisted they do the harbour cruise. It was impossible to refuse his generosity and the trip was certainly worth doing. Yet all she could think of, as she watched the sunset from the old elegant sailing junk, the soft breeze lifting her hair away from her face, was Jason and the desperate way he had kissed her that night in her room.

Christmas in Semarang didn't seem at all like Christmas. In the town it passed almost unnoticed, since most of the Javanese were Muslim, at least statistically. Plastic Christmas trees were available here and there, and in the larger stores 'I'm Dreaming of a White Christmas' and 'Rudolf the Rednosed Reindeer' could be heard playing over the PA system. The pavement shimmered with heat and Rae wondered if anybody here had any idea about snow and reindeer other than from magazine pictures. How strange it seemed to her not to have ever seen snow, much less played in it as she had as a child. But then, before she had come to Indonesia, she had never seen banana plants or mango trees and so many other new things.

She felt homesick for the first time. She talked with her mother and sister on the telephone, but it was a bad connection and it made the separation only seem worse. How much she longed now for home, the warmth and security she had known as a child. Log fires, apple pies, snow outside, the aroma of turkey roasting in the oven.

'We'll make our own Christmas,' Nicky said cheerfully. She had an endless supply of Christmas music and she played the tapes constantly while she was busy in the kitchen or wrapping presents. She had a large artificial tree, a beautiful one that seemed perfectly real, and together they decorated it with decorations Nicky had brought from home.

'We went home for Christmas last year,' she said. 'It was so wonderful, but so-oo cold. I had forgotten how cold it gets in Nebraska. And of course we had no clothes worth mentioning, so we wore borrowed coats and trousers and sweaters. It was really weird carrying all this stuff around on my body.' She laughed, tucking a strand of hair back into the untidy bun at the back of her head. 'But we had a lot of fun with my nephews and nieces playing in the snow.' She gazed pensively at the tree. 'It would be nice to have kids. We're going to be thinking about that one of these days.'

'After you're famous, of course,' Rae commented.

Nicky laughed. 'Of course.'

Despite the heat, Christmas was a festive day with twenty people arriving for a traditional turkey dinner. Ibu didn't mind at all working and helping with the dinner, as long as she could slip out at the prescribed times and do her prayers to Allah in her room. She had come to work wearing dress clothes and with her hair all done up, smiling happily.

It was before dinner, while everyone was having a pre-dinner drink, that David told Rae that Jason and Anouk were waiting to see her in the living-room. 'They've got a present for you.' He grinned. 'It's huge.'

It was the last thing she had wanted—a present from Jason. Oh, please, she moaned inwardly, no presents. Why couldn't he just leave her alone? Why did he have to make it so hard on her?

She went into the living-room, gathering her strength and resolve. She stood in the doorway, seeing Anouk dressed in another pretty dress, her hand resting on a large package next to her. Her eyes gleamed with pleasure and anticipation. Jason stood next to her, hands in his pockets.

'Merry Christmas, Rae.'

She swallowed hard. 'Merry Christmas.'

'We have a present for you,' Anouk announced unnecessarily. 'And I know you like it.' Carefully she pushed the package over the floor towards Rae.

'It was very nice to think about me, thank you, Anouk.' She began to rip off the paper, already guessing what it was from the chirping that came from inside.

A roomy rattan cage with two tiny green birds. She smiled delightedly. 'This is beautiful, Anouk, thank you.' She gave the girl a hug, which she accepted willingly. Holding her, Rae felt a surge of joy at the knowledge that Anouk had made such a surprising changeover. It had all been worth it. The warm hug was her best Christmas gift yet.

'I knew you would like it because you told us you had birds once and I remembered it.'

'That was very thoughtful.' She'd planned to go to the bird market and buy herself some birds for her small veranda, but she had not got around to it yet. 'And it's perfect. I'll put them on my veranda near the window so I can hear them in the morning when I wake up.' She smiled. 'And I have a present for you, too,' she said. 'Let me get it.'

Anouk was delighted with the lacquer box. 'It's perfect for my earrings!' she said. 'How did you know?'

'I saw your earrings. I thought you might like this to put them in.' Rae got another hug, and over the little girl's head her eyes met Jason's. She felt a sickening lurch in her stomach. His face was taut with grief and his blue eyes were dull with desolation.

The SICO had organised a New Year's Eve party at the Kelly house, complete with dinner, snacks and drinks—traditional foods produced by the various members of the community. Rae managed to avoid Jason, who came late, and after dinner was over she helped the *pembantu* in the kitchen, clearing away the dishes and talking to one of the Indian women who promised to give her a cooking lesson.

'Here you are.' Kevin stepped into the kitchen. 'Playing Cinderella?'

She laughed. 'Just helping out.'

'Well, here's the prince to take you to the ball.' He propelled her out of the door and into the enormous living-room that had been cleared for dancing. He swung her into his arms and they danced away.

'Have you heard about your Singapore job yet?' she asked, and he nodded.

'I'm not taking it. My company offered me a better contract if I stay for another year, so I took it. I have more autonomy here. I can do pretty much what I want.'

'I thought you were ready for a change.'

He shrugged. 'There's always next year. I do like it here, and besides, what would you do without me?'

She nodded. 'True. All alone, far away from home in a strange land. It's pathetic.'

He swung her around. 'Of course, you could come to Singapore with me.'

'I wouldn't be allowed to work there, and besides, they already speak English there.'

'True.' He sighed heavily. 'Well, so much for that scheme.'

'Scheme?'

He grinned. 'I'm not much good at sweeping you off your feet on to my white horse, but I was thinking I could possibly sweep you off by plane to some new and exotic place.'

'Java is exotic. I'm happy right here; no sweeping necessary.'

'Are you?' His arm tightened around her as he moved her away, out through the open door on to the moonlit lawn. 'You don't seem that happy to me, lately.' He studied her face and there was no laughter in his eyes.

She shrugged. 'I'm all right, don't worry about me.'

'But I do. I care about you, Rae, you know that.'

She nodded. 'I do, but there's nothing you can do.'

'I wish there was.' He lowered his face to hers and kissed her. It took her completely by surprise. She couldn't believe what was happening and she stood in his arms, totally thrown off guard.

There was sudden applause. 'Bravo!' came a voice.

They drew apart. Half a dozen people stood by the open doors, watching them, laughing.

Kevin straightened and grinned. 'You liked that, did you?' he asked them. His presence of mind astounded her.

'Encore! Encore!' one of the spectators called.

'My pleasure.' Before she knew what was happening, Kevin had bent her backwards over his arm in a book-cover-illustration pose and was kissing her again. Another round of applause followed. '*Bellissimo!*' one of them said.

Kevin straightened her into a vertical position again, placed her hand in the crook of his arm and regally walked her past the onlookers back into the house.

'How about a drink?' he asked.

She grimaced. 'Do you have to ask?'

'I hope I didn't embarrass you,' he said. 'I don't know what came over me.'

'It's all this prince stuff you were talking about. It went to your head.'

He laughed. 'That must have been it. However, I have the very distinct feeling it's not meant to be.'

'What isn't?'

'You and me.' He sighed dramatically. 'It seems like such a nice idea. We're such good friends.'

She laughed. 'That's probably why.'

'I keep thinking how nice it would be, you and me, together.'

She shook her head. 'It would never work. You're not madly, passionately in love with me. It's one of my many requirements.'

'So you want to be difficult about this, do you?' He gave her a narrow-eyed look.

She smiled sweetly up at him. 'Impossible, actually.'

He nodded. 'I was afraid of that.' He turned to the barman. 'Something strong and delicious for the lady.'

They sat down, joining a small group of people telling some hair-raising witchcraft stories from Africa. One thing you could be sure of in this group, the conversation was never boring.

She didn't have much time to relax before someone else asked her to dance. It was close to midnight when Jason took her hand and swung her on to the dance-floor. She went rigid in his arms.

'Relax,' he said. 'I don't bite.'

She gritted her teeth and looked away from him.

'That was quite a performance,' he said. 'You and Kevin.'

'I'm glad you enjoyed it,' she said caustically.

'I didn't, actually. Are you aware he has a woman in Yogya?'

She wasn't. It didn't matter, but she wondered why Kevin had never mentioned her. She kept her face straight, not wanting to give Jason the satisfaction of her surprise.

'That's interesting,' she said coolly, trying to keep as much space as possible between their bodies, which wasn't easy as he was determined to hold her close.

'I thought so, too.'

She strained against his hold, gritting her teeth.

'Stop fighting me,' he ordered on a low note. 'Relax. I have the feeling I'm dancing with a plastic Barbie doll.'

'I'll relax when I'm damn well ready! And it's not likely to be when you're around!' She only barely managed to keep her voice from rising. She wasn't anxious to draw attention to the two of them just now. 'If you don't like dancing with me, then do me a favour and let me go!'

'I have no intention of letting you go.' He sounded supremely confident and the words echoed in her head like a prophecy. He wasn't talking about dancing, and he knew that she understood.

His confident manner infuriated her, or was it something else? Was it really the fear that he was right that made her angry? The fear that she might not be able to stand up to him? When he was close like this, everything screamed inside her to give in to him, to let him hold her, to forget there was a past.

When the music stopped, he kept his arm around her and led her outside.

'I'm not going outside with you.'

His arm drew her closer in response. 'Yes, you are,' he said curtly. 'What I want to say to you nobody needs to hear. And if you want to scream your head off, go right ahead.'

She didn't want to scream her head off, and he knew it. She wasn't that hysterical, yet. He took her to a stand of bamboo, away from the doors and the lights. The moon was hidden behind the palm fronds and deep, dark shadows surrounded them.

'What do you want to talk about?' she asked, her voice coldly polite. 'Say your piece and let's get this over with.' She didn't like being here in the dark with him, with the sensuous whisperings of the bamboo leaves overhead and the velvety touch of the warm breeze stirring her hair and the bare skin of her arms.

He didn't say anything; instead he pulled her close against his body and kissed her. He kissed her hard and long and with a passion that made her tremble. All her anger simply vanished, as if swept away on a strong, warm wind. She couldn't think. She could only feel the strength of his body, the urgency of his mouth and hands. A need, vast and sweeping, made her body quiver.

When he released her, she almost fell. She couldn't feel her feet. It took her an endless moment to recover, then cold anger ran through her.

'You said you wanted to talk!' she whispered fiercely.

His mouth quirked. 'I decided actions speak louder than words.'

He was right. Nothing he could have said could have made her feel like this. She had no defences against his touch. All her hidden yearnings came rushing to the surface, and he knew it.

Would it ever go away? How could she live, for the rest of her life, with all this aching, painful longing. . .longing for something that wasn't even there? Jason wasn't the man she'd thought he was. All this pain for an illusion. She should have known. She should never have hoped so desperately for love. And in her mind she saw Kate shaking her head, heard her voice: *I told you so!*

From across the lawn, inside the house, came a burst of cheering, and then *Auld Lang Syne* erupted on the stereo and all were singing. It was twelve midnight.

'Happy New Year, Rae,' Jason said.

She stared at him, fighting with herself. I can't not wish him a happy New Year. *I can't.*

'Happy New Year,' she said, and her voice broke and tears ran down her face.

'I'm sorry,' he said softly. 'Please, Rae, give me a chance, for me, for yourself.'

'No,' she sobbed. 'No!' She whirled around and ran across the lawn back to the light and the music. At the open doors she took a deep breath and wiped her face. For several moments she stood quite still, regaining her control, then slowly she moved inside, took a glass of champagne from a tray and mingled with the cheerful crowd. With a desolate heart and a smile on her face she made the rounds, wishing everyone a very Happy New Year.

'Rae, it's so terrible, I don't know what to do first, where to begin.'

Rae had never seen Nicky so upset. Her eyes were wide, her face pale. She gestured with her hands wildly in all directions. Fear filled her. Something terrible had happened.

'Nicky, what's wrong?'

Tears filled Nicky's eyes. 'Dave's father, his brother, they died.'

'Oh, no,' Rae whispered. 'How awful! What happened?'

'They were in a plane, one of those little ones. It crashed in a thunderstorm. I don't know. Nobody knows, except that they're dead.'

Nicky looked around wildly. 'We're going to have to leave. Dave will have to go home to run the business. His brother was going to take over from his father, you know, but now. . .' She looked at Rae helplessly. 'I feel terrible, but I don't want to leave here. I don't want to live in Florida. I hate that place. It's all plastic and fake and. . .Oh, God, what am I talking about? I shouldn't be thinking about myself now, should I?' She covered her face with her hands. 'I don't know what to do,' she moaned.

It was a difficult, confusing time, and Rae tried as much as possible to help Nicky and David get organised. David flew back to the States immediately to help his mother and to take charge of the situation. He would be back in a week to spend another month handing over his job to a replacement. Somehow he had to make sure the business in Florida would survive without him for a month. The problems were mind-boggling.

Rae helped Nicky pack. Friends were in and out, trying to be of assistance. Rae had to find another place to live, or rather the school-board had to find her one. According to her contract, housing would be provided. There was no money to rent an entire house for her.

It was Kevin who came up with the solution. He didn't at all mind sharing his house with her. There was plenty of room and he was away half the time anyway, so she would have the place to herself.

All the members of the board voted yes, except Jason. Nobody asked for his reason; they all knew.

A week before Rae was due to move in with Kevin, Nicky and Rae were sitting on the veranda drinking gin and tonic when Jason came to the house. Nicky invited him in and mixed him a drink too. Rae felt tension take over her body. Her muscles grew rigid, and she stared out over the kampong below, avoiding Jason's gaze. The three of them sat in the gathering dusk, listening to the monotonous chanting coming from a nearby mosque, not a sound that was likely to lift the spirits.

'I just came from Sudiarto and it's all organised,' Jason said to Nicky. 'I'm taking over your lease, and I've let my own go.'

'Good,' Nicky said. She clearly didn't care. Housing was the company's responsibility and she had more important things to worry about than a broken lease.

'It's a bigger yard for Anouk,' he said, 'and she's been begging me for a dog. We can't have one in the place we have now.'

Nicky sighed. 'At least now I'll know who lives here. It won't seem so strange thinking about it.' She bit her lip. 'Five years in the same place is a long time.'

'Too long, some people say.'

'Not for me. I like it here. I don't need Florida.' Her
mouth curved in a humourless smile. 'Who needs safe
drinking water and microwave ovens?'

'There's always Disney World if you need cheering
up.'

Nicky gave Jason a withering look and he laughed.
'Anouk is already talking about visiting you.'

'You're always welcome, of course. As a matter of
fact, the more visitors, the better.' She got up from her
chair. 'I have to talk to Ibu. I'll be right back.'

Alone with Jason, Rae grew even tenser. She
anchored herself in the chair as if she were afraid he
would blast her out of it. She focused on a potted palm
and sipped her drink.

'Rae, I wish you'd stay on in the guest apartment
here.'

She jerked her head sideways to look at him. 'No. I
have a perfectly good place to go to.'

'Staying here would be easier.'

'No, it wouldn't.' She clenched her hands into fists.
'You didn't really think I would stay here with you in
the same house, did you?'

He smiled ruefully. 'No. But hope springs eternal.'
There was self-derision in his voice. 'I keep thinking
that one day you're going to come to the conclusion
that I'm not the despicable character you think I am.'

If only that could be true, she thought bitterly, but it
wasn't. It never could be. She could never forgive him.
Never.

Nicky came back and sat down. 'I think I've found
Ibu a job with that Australian couple that just moved
in. She's going for an interview tomorrow. What about
the nightwatchman?' she asked Jason. 'Do you keep
your own?'

He shook his head. 'Mine goes with the house. The
owners pay him. If yours wants to stay on here, I'll
gladly keep him. That is, if he's any good.'

'In five years we've never been robbed.'

'That's as good a recommendation as I need.' He got up from his chair. 'I think I'd better get back for dinner.'

'I wish you two could kiss and make up,' Nicky said after he'd gone. 'He's crazy about you, you know, and he's miserable.' She waved her hand in dismissal. 'But then half the human race is miserable, so maybe in the cosmic scene it's not important. What's happiness but a fleeting illusion?'

Rae groaned and then, despite everything, she laughed. 'Oh, Nicky, melodrama is not your style. Not even Florida can be that depressing.'

'Have you ever been there?'

'No.'

Nicky grimaced. 'I thought not.'

A week before Nicky and David were due to leave, Rae moved in with Kevin. It was a depressing time. She was going to miss them, and she felt sorry for Nicky, who was miserable at the prospect of living in Florida. David seemed a different person, silent and morose, with his usual jovial manner and silly jokes gone.

A number of friends gathered at the airport to see the Kings off. Jason and Anouk were there, too. Every time Rae saw Jason, she was aware of her heart doing crazy things, of her blood rushing faster, of the pain digging itself deeper into her heart. Why couldn't she just stay calm and indifferent when she saw him? She didn't want him. She hated him. She could never forgive him. She kept repeating it in her mind over and over again, but nothing seemed to change. All she needed was to set eyes on him and her emotions went wild.

A tearful Nicky kissed everyone goodbye, and Rae couldn't help but think how much it was like her and Matt's goodbye when they had left Semarang. But she had come back, and maybe Nicky and David, too, would come back again.

Nothing is forever, Kate would say. You've got to make your own luck; don't let fate take over too much.

Fate, she thought, as she and Kevin left the airport. What was Fate? Fate had brought her and Matt to Indonesia. Fate had brought her Jason.

She realised that Kevin was asking her something and she hadn't heard a word he'd said.

'I'm sorry, what did you say?'

'Let's go and have something to eat and see a movie.'

'That would be nice, thanks.'

He gave her a searching look. 'What were you thinking about?'

'Fate.'

'Yeah, it's a bitch.' He sounded very Australian, and she smiled. It would be a change not having Nicky to talk to any more, but it would be all right staying with Kevin.

It all went quite smoothly. Kevin was away a lot of the time and she felt lonely in the big house. She gave a couple of dinner parties, had tea with Hillie once a week, and started teaching an adult class on Tuesday afternoons. She kept herself quite busy, yet the aching emptiness didn't go away. No amount of work could fill that emptiness. She kept dreaming about Jason, waking up in tears. She had trouble falling asleep and would lie awake for hours.

I'm going to have to do something, she thought desperately one evening. Somehow I've got to get him out of my system. It was almost one o'clock and she'd been in bed for two hours, listening to the torrential rain that had been coming down for hours now.

She gave a groan of exasperation, then crawled out of bed and went to the kitchen. Maybe a snack and some hot tea would help. She waited for the water to boil and poured it on the tea. The rain had stopped,

and through the open window came only the soft sound
of dripping foliage. She set the kettle down on the
stove and cut herself a piece of pineapple coconut cake
that the cook had made.

Noise thundered through the air, and she started so
violently that the knife fell from her hand and dropped
on to the counter. The house shook, the glasses on the
bar in the living-room rattled. She stood frozen in
sudden terror, the ground vibrating under her feet, the
deafening noise filling her head, her mind. She had
never heard such all-obliterating noise. Never felt the
ground shake and shudder under her feet. She didn't
know whether to stand still or run. She couldn't think.
Wildly she looked around. Any moment now the walls
would come crashing in on her, burying her alive. Panic
surged through her. I've got to get out of here! she
thought. *I've got to get out of here!*

Then the lights went out.

CHAPTER NINE

ALL was dark; a deep, oppressing blackness. For a terrifying moment it seemed as though Rae's heart had stopped beating. She couldn't see. *She couldn't see!* For an agonising instant she was five again, afraid of tigers under the bed, ghosts in the wardrobe, spiders on her pillow. Then suddenly all was silent. A dangerous, deadly silence. Her nerves jumped, tiny pinpricks all over her skin. She was shaking so hard that she couldn't make her legs move. Her heart was pumping in a terrifying rhythm and she clutched her arms in front of her chest as if to hold it inside. She closed her eyes, taking a deep breath, trying to calm her shattered nerves.

The eerie silence continued. No rain, no wind. Nothing. Carefully, hands held out in front of her like a blind person, she moved to the kitchen door leading to the outside. She felt with her hands for the knob and turned it. The door wouldn't move. With trembling fingers she searched for the key. It was in the lock, but it wasn't turned. She pushed at the door again, but it wouldn't budge. The door was blocked. She broke out in a cold sweat.

She would have to get out through the front door. She only hoped it wasn't blocked as well. Hair-raising visions of being trapped in the empty black house made her legs move forward, out of the kitchen. What had happened? An earthquake? Some horrible explosion? She sniffed the air, but smelled only damp earth and green, growing things. Where was the watchman? Why wasn't anybody here? Why didn't she hear anything?

The telephone! She touched the cool surface of the

refrigerator, and groped for the telephone to the left of
it on the wall. She lifted the receiver and put it to her
ear. Nothing. Dead. Fear clutched at her throat. Move!
she told herself. Get out of here!

Carefully she shuffled into the dining-room. Her
eyes were getting used to the dark, and in the faint
light from the moon that sneaked through the window
she could make out the shapes of the furniture.

She peered out of the window, wondering what had
happened, if there was anything to see. In the ghostly
glow of a half-moon, the devastation was shocking.
The entire back yard had been transformed into a
desolate moonscape of rocks and rubble. The veranda
had gone, the car port had gone. Water streamed down
the driveway, bringing with it mud and debris.

The twelve-foot stone retaining wall had come down,
tons of rock crashing down the sloped garden, taking
with it the electrical wiring attached to it.

She took another steadying breath. It was not an
earthquake, not an aeroplane crashing into the yard. It
was over. The house was still standing. She was not
hurt. She made a hasty step to reach the birdcage, and
retreated to the front of the house.

The front door opened easily, and outside, in the
front garden, all was normal and serene. Dazed, she
stared out into the night. She couldn't think of what to
do next. A group of people had gathered near the gate,
the neighbourhood night watchmen and their hangers-
on.

The ordeal had seemed to last an eternity, yet she
realised that in actual fact it had taken but a minute for
the wall to come crashing down.

A car came screeching down the road. A man
jumped out and the watchman opened the gates for
him.

'Rae!' Jason came running up to the front door, a
huge torch in his hand.

'Thank God,' he said. 'You're all right.'

'The wall came down.'

'I know. I heard it. I was sitting on my veranda.' He was breathing hard, forcing the words out between breaths.

She was glad to see him, to see anybody, yet she wished it could have been someone else. She covered her feelings by putting the cage down safely in the porch.

He propelled her inside. 'Let's see the damage.'

'The whole back yard,' she said, 'the car port, my veranda.'

They went into her bedroom and he shone the torch around, over the window, the floor, the bed.

Her stomach turned over in shock. 'Oh, my God,' she whispered.

The window had been smashed by a flying rock, and glass covered the rumpled bed and floor. The rock lay on her pillow, as if neatly deposited there by a careful hand.

'You'd gone to bed already,' he said tonelessly.

She stared in horror at the bed, and her body began to tremble violently. 'I got up because I couldn't sleep.'

'You would have been dead,' he said, and his voice shook. In the muted light his face looked grey. His eyes bored into hers and the silence quivered between them. Then he hauled her to him, crushing her against him. He kissed her hard and long and desperately and she leaned weakly into him, having no strength to resist him.

He broke away, breathing heavily. 'You'd better come home with me,' he said. 'You can't stay here.'

No, she thought, dazed. No! I can't go home with him. She shook her head. 'I can sleep in the other bedroom.'

'No! Are you out of your mind? Only part of the

wall is down. The rest could go any moment. And you've got no electricity. You're coming with me.'

She had no choice but to follow him out to his car and be driven around the corner to his house. She hugged herself, feeling cold and shaken, shivering despite the hot, humid night.

She would stay in the guest apartment, the place where she had lived when Nicky and David had still lived in the house. It would be all right. Tomorrow Kevin would come home and something could be figured out.

She couldn't stop shivering, and he took her into the living-room and poured her a drink.

'This should calm you down.'

She took the glass from him and drank the Scotch. She hated the stuff, but it worked. She sank down on the sofa, pulled up her legs and rested her head on her knees.

'Why were you sitting on the veranda in the dead of night?' she asked.

'Probably for the same reason you were in the kitchen in the dead of night,' he said drily. 'I couldn't sleep. So I just sat there. I can see the west side of Kevin's house, and when I heard the noise I knew it had to come from there. Where is he, by the way?'

She shrugged. 'On a trip. To Cerabon or Solo, I don't know. Maybe he's in Yogya with his girlfriend.'

He gave her an odd look and she sighed wearily. 'I don't care if he has a hundred women. For whatever it's worth, there's nothing between him and me. There never was. We're just friends.' She wasn't sure why she said it, except that this didn't seem to be the time for silly games and pretences. A heavy rock lay on her pillow and she could have been dead.

Jason said nothing and poured himself another drink.

Her body felt deadly tired, yet her mind was wide awake. 'I'll never sleep again,' she said dully.

'Not for the rest of your life?' She could hear the amusement in his voice.

'Probably. All I can hear is that horrible noise. I felt the ground shaking. It was the most terrifying experience. I can imagine what people go through in an earthquake.' She shuddered. She lifted her head and drank the rest of the Scotch, a little too fast.

He sat down next to her and wrapped his arms around her. 'Let me hold you,' he said in her hair.

'No,' she said.

'Yes.'

She didn't fight. She had no fight in her. She felt drained and frightened and she kept seeing the rock on her pillow. She couldn't stop shivering.

He stroked her hair as if she were a child. 'It's all right,' he said quietly. 'It's over.'

Slowly but surely, the Scotch eased the shaking. Her body began to calm down. She was tired, so tired and she didn't want to move. It felt good and safe in his arms, so comforting to feel the warmth of his body against hers, chasing the cold from her bones.

An endless time later, or maybe it was only minutes, he slowly released her.

'You're falling asleep,' he said quietly. 'You'd better get to bed.' He drew her to her feet and gently ushered her out of the door to the guest bedroom. She stared at the bed, neatly made, and it looked cold and empty and she felt so utterly lonely that it brought tears to her eyes.

'What's wrong?' he asked.

Her throat closed and she shook her head, tears coming down her cheeks. She didn't know why she was crying, why she kept seeing the rock on her pillow, why she couldn't get a grip on herself and be rational. But all she wanted, really wanted, was Jason's arms around her. She didn't want to be alone.

He drew her to him with a groan. 'Oh, God, Rae,' he muttered. 'Please don't cry.'

She clung to him, and he kissed her open mouth, her wet cheeks. She wanted to think of nothing else and she let him take her into his own room, into his own bed. He held her until all the cold was gone and a slow, lazy fire warmed her inside. There was no time and no place, no past and no future. There was only now and the need for the comfort of his big, warm body.

His hands roamed over her and his kisses grew wilder and hungrier and the fire inside her burned with increasing heat. She was no longer tired. A yearning, deep and aching, made her turn to him, hold him, touch him in turn.

No words were needed. They knew a language more eloquent than any spoken tongue, a language of love and desire, of giving and taking, of infinite sweetness and unsurpassed fulfilment.

Rae awoke in the morning, stretching luxuriously, smiling to herself, feeling a delicious sense of well-being. It wasn't until she'd come to full consciousness that she understood the reason.

She opened her eyes, realising that she was not in her own bed and that Jason was sleeping next to her. Her heart began to race, and then a terrible anger overwhelmed her when everything came back to her. The wall, Jason, making love.

She slipped out of bed noiselessly and put on her nightgown and robe. She'd come without her clothes last night. How was she going to go back home in broad daylight without her clothes on?

The bed creaked. 'Good morning, Rae.'

She turned to face him, but she found no words. Hands behind his head, hair dishevelled, he looked at her with a smile. 'Come back to bed.'

'No!' Her voice shook.

'Are you all right?'

'No, I'm not all right! What a rotten thing to do,' she said fiercely. 'What a *rotten* thing to do!'

Surprise flashed across his face. 'What?'

'You know what! You took advantage of me! You took advantage of my being upset and scared so you could get me into bed!'

He sat straight up in bed, his jaw hard and tensed. 'Rae,' he said, his voice calm with terrible control, 'don't give me that!'

'Why not? It's true, isn't it?'

He gave a humourless laugh. 'What did you expect of me? You didn't want to be alone. You were shaken and crying. You wanted to sleep with me, and don't you dare deny it! Am I supposed to be in complete control at all times? I needed you, I wanted you, you're right. But you needed me, too. You wanted me; don't tell me you didn't! And for God's sake don't act like you're sixteen and I took your virginity!'

She winced at the harshness of his words, knew she had deserved the accusation. She knew he was right, there was no use in denying she hadn't wanted to stay with him last night. But now, in the clear light of morning, everything was different and she felt angry, deeply angry, but it was directed as much at herself as at him. She didn't want to want him, she didn't want to love him. She didn't, she *didn't*! She could never love him.

She said nothing; she had no reply. Their eyes met and held in the silence. Then he got out of bed and took her in his arms. 'I love you,' he said softly. 'Rae, I love you.'

His body, warm and naked, made her heart pound. 'No,' she said fiercely. 'No!' She pulled herself away, tears blinding her. 'Don't you dare say that!'

'Why not? It's true.'

She didn't know what to think any more. She

couldn't think. There was only the pain and confusion of her thoughts—anger and sadness and the terrible sense of betrayal.

'Why not?' he repeated. 'Why can't I say I love you?'

'Because I don't love you!' she cried. She saw the pain in his eyes, felt her own heart tear in anguish. 'Don't you understand? *I don't love you!*'

She didn't know how long she'd sat on the veranda after she'd fled the bedroom when Jason came to her.

'There are some clothes in the guest bedroom,' he said evenly. 'You can get dressed. Breakfast is in twenty minutes.'

'I don't want breakfast.'

He didn't argue with her. 'Some coffee, then?'

'Please.' She swallowed hard. 'What about Anouk? What will you tell her?'

'She's still in her room, dressing. I'll tell her the truth. The wall came down and damaged your house and you spent the night here.'

She nodded. 'OK.'

She showered and dressed. Her clothes were on the bed; a blue-green flowered dress, white panties, a white bra, blue sandals. Had he gone through her wardrobe and drawers himself? Probably. Well, he'd been a married man once. The sight of women's clothes probably didn't bother him a whole lot.

So why did it bother her to know he had gone through her things? She didn't want this closeness, this intimacy with him. Yet they had made love last night; how much more intimate could they get?

And he loved her. He said he loved her.

Tears burned behind her eyes and her stomach cramped. She covered her face with her hands and sank down on to the bed with a moan of despair.

*   *   *

Eyes sparkling, Anouk looked from Jason to Rae.

'This is very fun!' she said, giving a little bounce in her chair. Dressed in a cheerful yellow dress, she sat at the breakfast table, bright as a May flower. 'I like visitors.' She frowned and looked apologetically at Rae. 'But I'm sorry your house is broken.'

Rae nodded. 'I know what you mean,' she said reassuringly.

'You can stay here with us, can't she, Papa? You lived here before, didn't you? And then we moved here. And the other house, you lived there too, Papa told me. With your husband. He died, didn't he?'

'Yes, he did.'

'Eat your breakfast, Anouk,' Jason said, his voice short.

Anouk glanced down at her bread and cheese and sighed. 'I'm not hungry.'

Rae sipped her coffee. She wasn't hungry, either. Her nerves were strung so tight she was afraid something might snap. She took the platter of sliced fruit and offered it to Anouk.

'Maybe you'd like some fruit. It's important to eat in the mornings.'

'*You're* not eating,' Anouk pointed out, reluctantly taking a small slice of mango.

Rae managed a smile. 'I'll have some fruit.' She helped herself to a wedge of papaya and a slice of fresh pineapple.

'Fruit alone is not enough, that's what Papa says. I always have to have bread and cheese or an egg or cereal. He says I need egg white, don't you, Papa?'

'Protein,' he corrected. 'You should be eating instead of talking. You'll be late for school if you don't hurry up now.'

Jason, obviously, was in no mood for cheerful conversation. Anouk sulked and ate her food, albeit reluctantly.

Rae got up from the table. 'Thank you for breakfast,' she said to Jason. 'If you'll excuse me now, I'll go to the house and get my bag.'

He nodded, his eyes expressionless.

Rae ruffled Anouk's hair. 'I'll see you at school in a little while.'

When she got back to the house, she couldn't believe her eyes. In the daylight the devastation looked even worse. The entire back yard was strewn with rock and rubble, the flowering bushes crushed beneath the tons of stones.

Inside, the *pembantu* was already cleaning up the glass and debris in Rae's room.

Rae wished her good morning and looked dully at the mess.

'You were lucky,' the girl said in Indonesian, her dark eyes looking meaningfully at the stripped bed.

Rae spent some time relaying the story of the disaster to the girl, although she was sure she'd already heard the details in Technicolor from the night watchman when she'd come to work this morning. The night watchman was still around, clearing the driveway so Kevin could at least park his Landcruiser inside the gates when he returned in the afternoon.

The home-owner would have to be notified, and Rae didn't know who he was, but it could probably wait till Kevin came back. Until the damages were repaired she could move into one of the other bedrooms.

Once in school she had to go over everything again, as Anouk had informed everybody that the teacher had slept at her house because her own had been completely destroyed in a terrible accident in the middle of the night.

It was not one of her better mornings.

'I should have known this would happen one day,' Kevin said, furiously slamming his fist into the open palm of his other hand. 'It's the most idiotic wall anybody ever built. They didn't fill it in with dirt behind it, just left it there, and the water ran right along it, which was fine most of the time, but not last night.'

'What happened, then?'

'Too much build-up. It didn't flow off quickly enough and the pressure became too much and poof.' He gave her a pained look. 'You could have been killed.'

'I was lucky.'

He sighed heavily. 'God, I can't believe this. Where am I when you really need me?'

'In Yogya with your girlfriend,' she said without thinking.

His eyes widened in surprise. 'How do you know about her?'

'Was it a big secret?'

He shrugged. 'Not particularly.'

'Everybody knows everything in Semarang,' she said, making a face. 'So tell me, what's her name, who is she?'

He shrugged. 'Her name is Tarida. She's Indonesian and she teaches mathematics at the university.'

'Why didn't you ask her to go to Singapore with you? Why don't you ask her to marry you?'

He looked at her darkly. 'She won't have me. Besides, I'm never getting married again.'

'Oh, yes, I remember now.' She laughed. 'We'll just wait and see.'

He kicked a small rock and it went careening down the sloped driveway. 'You stayed at Jason's last night, did you say?'

She nodded. 'He heard the noise. He was still awake, so he came to the rescue.'

'Is there anything between the two of you that I should understand?'

No, she wanted to say, there's nothing, but it would

be a lie. Whatever it was, it was not nothing, and Jason
knew it well enough. Last night they'd made love, and
that most certainly had not been nothing. 'I don't want
to talk about it,' she said miserably.

'Are you in love with him?'

Her body tensed and her hands clenched into fists.
'No,' she said.

His eyes narrowed. 'Are you sure?'

'Of course I'm sure! Now what kind of question is
that? And it isn't any of your business, is it?'

He shrugged. 'No, it's not, except that I'm worried
about you. You're my friend, and I can worry about
my friend, can't I?'

'I'm sorry,' she murmured, regretting her outburst.
'This whole thing just made me jumpy. I didn't mean
to be rude.'

He patted her hand. 'Forget it.' Then he grinned. 'If
for whatever reason you'd want me to beat him up,
just say the word.'

'Kevin!'

He laughed out loud. 'I'd better phone the landlord.'

The sun was fierce and hot, but in the shade it felt
quite comfortable. Rae lay stretched out on a lounger,
listening to the noises of the children playing in the
pool. Sunday morning was a favourite time to be at the
Patra Jasa pool, and Rae enjoyed talking with her
friends, lazing in the sun and taking a dip now and then
when she got too hot.

'You want some more lemonade?' Hillie asked,
holding up the Thermos she'd brought from home.
With four kids, she wasn't about to buy the drinks from
the hotel. They were all in the pool now, playing with
Joost, who seemed to have an endless repertoire of
silly games.

'If you've got some.' Rae sat up, squinting at the
bright sky. She took the plastic cup that Hillie handed

her. 'Thanks. I'll buy the gang some ice-cream after a while, if you don't object.'

'You don't have to.'

'I know.' She tried not to look at Jason, who was sitting at the next umbrella table talking to three Americans she didn't know, although one of them seemed vaguely familiar. It was hard to pretend they weren't there; she could hear their voices quite clearly. They were talking business.

'Who are those guys with Jason?' she asked Hillie. 'Any idea?'

Hillie shrugged. 'They used to work for him, or with him, or something. They're here doing a feasibility study for some project or other. Shrimp. Or was it rattan furniture? Something like that.'

Rae laughed. 'Something like that.'

'Hey, what do I know? He and Joost sat up all night talking business, and I didn't understand half of it so I went to bed.' She blew at her fringe and waved her hand like a fan in front of her face. 'I'm going in for a swim. I'm cooked.'

'You look cooked. You'd better watch out.'

Hillie rolled her eyes. 'Yes, Mother.'

'You can dish it out, but you can't take it, right?'

Hillie gave a puzzled frown. 'What do you mean, dish it out?'

'Serve it up. Hand it out. You can give warnings, but you don't like taking them.'

Hillie groaned. 'God, I'll never learn English.'

Rae laughed. 'You're a hopeless case, for sure. Now get your hide in the water, before it turns to leather.'

Rae followed her a moment later, aware of Jason's eyes on her, wishing he would just pack up and go home so that she wouldn't have to see him or hear his voice.

The swim cooled her off nicely and she sat back on her lounger, not drying off, and picked up her book.

She glanced up some time later, when the sun hit her legs. Jason and Anouk had gone. Joost was sitting next to Hillie, reading a Dutch news magazine. She got up to push the lounger further into the shade, which moved her closer to the men still sitting around the table drinking beer.

The kids were climbing out of the pool, begging for something and getting a firm shake of the head from their mother.

'How about some ice-cream?' Rae asked.

A cheer went up. Rae gave them all some money and they trooped off to the far end of the pool to get it.

Rae lay back and closed her eyes, thinking drowsily that it would be nice to take a nap right here, but the voices of the men at the next table were too loud, and their laughter irritated her.

'I don't know that we can duplicate the IPD project,' one of them was saying. 'I know Grant seems to think it's worth looking into, but. . .'

The Industrial Park Development Project. The project Matt had worked on. She was no longer drowsy. Well, what did she care? They could duplicate it a hundred times and it would have nothing to do with her. She tried to block out the voices, and for a while she didn't hear much, just some isolated words.

'That Smith character. Man, oh, man did we have trouble!'

She jerked upright, her heart in her throat.

'Why?' one of the men asked.

'He was incompetent. Didn't listen to anybody. Didn't think he needed anybody's advice; he had the answers to everything.'

Blood drained from her face. More words, more sentences followed, like shards of glass hitting her consciousness. She couldn't move. Her body seemed frozen to the lounger as she listened to the men damning the man she had loved, the man who had been her husband.

'Rae? What's wrong?' The urgency in Hillie's voice stirred her out of her stupor.

She shook her head helplessly. Her throat felt like sandpaper and her tongue refused to form a syllable.

Hillie got up out of her chair. 'Rae! Are you sick? You look like death!'

Rae swallowed. 'I'm all right.' She forced the words out; her throat ached, her chest burned.

Hillie sat down on the end of Rae's lounger. 'Something's wrong! Are you sure you're feeling all right?' Hillie was not to be reassured. Her hand reached out and felt Rae's forehead. 'No fever.'

'I'm not sick.' She began to shake, belying her words. 'Really. It's these men.' She swallowed painfully. 'They were saying things about my husband.' She felt cold, so cold.

'Your *husband*?'

'They knew about the project he worked on three years ago. They were saying things. . .lies.'

As if in answer, a burst of laughter came from the next table. Then the shattering of glass as someone dropped a bottle. A curse erupted in the silence that followed.

Rae got up. 'Please, would you mind taking me home?'

'No, of course not.' Hillie gave her a worried look. 'People talk, you know. And it's so long ago. Maybe you didn't hear it right.'

'Oh, I heard it right.'

Hillie said something to Joost in Dutch and grabbed her bag. 'Let's go.'

Numbly, Rae gathered her things. Like a sleepwalker she followed Hillie out of the pool area, down the steps, past the hotel's beauty salon into the blazing car park. The white-hot sky made her eyes ache. Car bumpers glinted in the sun and the tarmac shimmered in the heat. She shivered. Inside her was a core of ice and she had never been so cold in her life.

She sat in the passenger's seat, staring blindly out of the window.

'Do you want to talk about it?' Hillie urged.

She shook her head. 'I. . .I have to think.' It was too painful to talk about, the words too sharp to form in her mouth, and she hugged the knowledge inside her like some terrible secret.

Hillie hadn't known Matt, had never met him— loving, laughing Matt with his warm brown eyes, his wonderful sense of humour.

It was only a few minutes to the house, and Hillie left her reluctantly at the gate. 'Phone me if you need me,' she said.

'Thank you, I will.'

Kevin, wrapped in a sarong, stood in the kitchen, brewing himself some *kopi tubruk*, pouring boiling water straight on to the ground coffee in a blue-flecked enamelled coffee-pot. By all appearances, he'd just got out of bed. His hair stood on end and he looked rather groggy. Not the picture of a prince ready to save the damsel in distress. And here I am, she thought, a damsel in distress.

'Morning,' he muttered. 'Back from the pool already?'

'It was too hot.' Not much of an excuse. It was always hot.

'Yeah. You want some coffee?'

'Please.' Maybe that was what she needed—some of that lethally strong brew that Kevin concocted. 'I'll put my stuff away. I'll be right back.'

In her room she took off her swimsuit and slipped into a pair of khaki shorts and a flowered shirt. She stood in front of the mirror and gazed at herself. She looked pale and old.

Lies, she thought. All lies.

It's a long time ago, Hillie had said. And she was right. Yet the knowledge didn't seem to help. Something terrible had happened right here in this town, and now Matt was dead. She had lost her husband because of the vicious lies of other people.

A short rap on the door startled her. 'Coffee's getting cold, love.'

The cook was off on Sundays and Kevin fixed them both some lunch a while later, but Rae couldn't get a bite past her throat. The coffee had brought Kevin back to consciousness and he regarded her with a frown.

'What happened at the pool?' he asked.

'Nothing. I just have a headache from the sun. I think I'll lie down for a while.' He knew she was lying, she could tell by the look in his eyes. For a moment she was tempted to tell him, yet more than anything she wanted to be alone now, to hide.

She closed the curtains against the white light. She turned on the air-conditioning unit, blocking out the world. No noise came in through the closed windows. She could not hear the birds in the cage or the sounds drifting up from the kampong below. There was only the hum of the air-conditioner and the haunting words echoing inside her head.

She lay on the bed, listening to the voices in her head, tears slowly dripping down her cheeks on to the pillow. She wasn't sure why she was crying—for Matt, for herself, for all the losses and sorrows that never seemed to end.

She would have to confront Jason and tell him what she knew. How did he dare think she could want him, knowing what she knew? How did they dare tell lies like that about Matt? Had Jason been part of this? Was this the way he had got rid of Matt?

For a long time she lay in the silent room. Then she came slowly to her feet. She went into the bathroom and washed her face and hands. Her reflection stared back at her with dull eyes. She looked washed out, but she had no energy to do anything about it. It didn't matter.

She took a deep breath and slowly let it out. There was no reason to wait, no reason to postpone.

She would go to see Jason now.

CHAPTER TEN

SAUDA, the cook, opened the door, smiling her silver-toothed smile. '*Pak* Jason is on the veranda,' she said in Indonesian. 'You can go.'

Delicious odours wafted in from the kitchen. Sauda was apparently cooking up a storm and eager to get back to her wok. '*Terima kasih*,' Rae said, trying to smile. It made her face feel as if it would shatter into splinters of ice.

Her heart in her throat, she walked through the familiar living-room, hearing voices coming from the veranda. Jason wasn't alone. Maybe the Moermans were here. What was she going to do now? She couldn't possibly join them and make friendly conversation.

She glanced through the large open doors, feeling a cold shiver go down her spine as she recognised the men from the hotel pool. They were having an animated conversation, drinking, laughing and eating crisp *krupuk* crackers from a huge bowl on the table.

Jason's chair faced the open doors and he saw her standing in the room before she had a chance to turn around and leave. He wore white shorts and a blue shirt that made his eyes look brighter than the sky.

He got to his feet, excused himself and came inside.

'Rae?' He seemed surprised to see her. She avoided him whenever possible and hadn't spoken to him for over a week now.

'I wanted to talk to you. I didn't know you had company.'

He searched her face, frowning. 'What's wrong?'

'I'll come back another time.'

'No.' He took her arm and propelled her out of the

177

living-room into his office. 'You're shaking. Are you all right? Tell me.'

No! she wanted to scream. I'm not all right! But the words stuck in her throat like hard, cold pebbles and she swallowed hard. 'You have to go back to your visitors,' she said nervously, her courage failing her. 'You can't just leave them.'

'I can do any damn thing I please!' he said impatiently. 'Rae, tell me what's wrong! Why are you so nervous?'

She twisted her hands together to keep them from trembling. 'Who are these men?'

He made an irritable gesture. 'Forget the men.'

'I need to know. I want to know.'

He stared at her for a moment. 'They're here from the States. Just for a couple of weeks, doing a feasibility study.'

'Who do they work for?'

'Global Development.'

'The company you worked for?'

He nodded. 'Right.'

'So you know these guys?'

He sighed heavily. 'Yes, I know them. They worked for me. One of them worked on the IPD project, overseeing it from Jakarta.'

'The bald one.' It had been the one who seemed vaguely familiar. Matt might have brought him home for lunch or a drink or something like that, when the man had been visiting from Jakarta.

He nodded. 'Greg Oldfield.' He frowned impatiently. 'Please tell me what this is all about.'

She bit her lip hard. 'This morning, at the pool, after you left, I heard them talking.' She took a deep breath, feeling the cold again, the chill running through her veins. 'They were talking about Matt, about the project. They were saying terrible things about him. All lies, vicious lies.' The anger was winning over her

nerves, rising to her head. She glared at him coldly.
'How did that ever happen? You tell me how these lies
ever came into circulation!'

'What was it they were saying?'

She clenched her fists. 'I'm sure you know! I'm sure
you must have started them!'

Anger leaped into his eyes. His mouth tightened and
his lower jaw hardened. 'I've listened to your innuen-
does and accusations long enough now. At least have
the decency to tell me exactly what they are!'

'Decency? You have the gall to talk about decency?
What you did to Matt was despicable!' She was shaking
so hard that she couldn't stand up any longer. She
grabbed the back of a chair for support.

'Rae, for God's sake, let's have a rational
discussion!'

'Rational?' He expected her to be rational when she
felt nothing but icy anger rushing through her system
without check.

He moved to the door. 'I'm getting you a drink.'

'I don't want a drink!' He left the room, but was
back only moments later. He handed her a glass. 'It's
Scotch. Drink it.'

'I don't need it!' She felt like throwing it in his face,
but all she did was stand there with the glass in her
hands and tears running down her face. Why was she
crying? Why was this terrible anger clogging her throat
and wrenching at her heart? She took a gulp from the
Scotch and it burned down her throat, but it didn't
melt the ice inside.

He put his hands back in his pockets and gave her a
steady look. He seemed to have calmed himself. 'Now
tell me what it was they were saying.'

She took another gulp of the whisky, wincing as it
went down. 'They said he was incompetent and nearly
ruined the project. It's the most vicious thing I've ever
heard! He worked all the time. He was breathing,

eating and sleeping the damn project! He wanted to do the best job possible. He always worked that way, no matter what he did!'

The Scotch wasn't working. She couldn't stop herself now. The words kept coming, as if someone else forced them out, past her throat and tongue and lips. 'He was a brilliant teacher! He graduated *magna cum laude*. His doctoral dissertation was used as a teaching book; how often does that happen? He was offered an associate professorship and he turned it down to come here! How dare they say he was incompetent? Is that the way you got rid of him, starting rumours? Lies?'

His eyes were full of blue fire. Anger tensed his muscles and she could see from the rigid lines of his body that he was doing his utmost to control his anger. His eyes bored into hers. 'No, Rae,' he said with icy calmness, 'that's not the way I got rid of him. I did not start rumours. I did not tell lies.'

'And I'm supposed to believe that?'

His mouth twisted bitterly. 'If you cared at all, you would at least try.' He turned his back on her, as if he could no longer stand the sight of her. He stared out of the window, the hands in his pockets balled into fists. 'Your husband was a very intelligent man and a very superior thinker,' he said in a tightly controlled voice. 'I've never denied that, and neither has anyone else I know.'

'Then you tell me why they were saying he was incompetent!'

Jason turned to face her. There was a stillness in the room, and a cold shiver went through her as he looked into her eyes.

'Because he was, Rae.'

Her body felt odd, with a light cold quivering all over. 'You're saying he was incompetent?'

He rubbed his forehead wearily. 'I'm sorry, Rae, but it's the truth.'

She shook her head. 'It can't be! I don't understand. Why are you saying that? How can you say that?' Her voice was high, as if it came from soneone else, someone over in the corner of the room.

'He wasn't the right man for this assignment, Rae. He should never have been offered this job, not this one.' He sighed heavily. 'We needed flexibility and creativity, and Matt, very clearly, was an academic. He lacked the ability to take his book knowledge and theories and integrate them creatively with the realities of the situation.' He raked his fingers through his hair. He looked tired and she noticed, for the first time, a touch of grey in his hair. He met her eyes and held her gaze. 'I am not attacking his character, Rae,' he said quietly. 'He was well intentioned, but he simply didn't have the right capabilities. We all have our different talents. We can't all do the same things right. He had a great mind, but we needed something else for this job. We couldn't let a twenty-million-dollar development project go down the tubes because we wanted to be nice and not hurt his feelings.'

Inside her everything had stilled, as if a storm had quieted its raging. His words settled in her mind, finding no surprise, no opposition. The truth, she thought. It's the truth. Maybe she'd known all along that there was a different truth, another reality.

Slowly she sat down on a chair, her head bent. It was hard to breathe. The air seemed too thick, smelling of dust. She rubbed her arms. Her skin felt as dry as paper. 'Couldn't you have explained it to him? If he had such a great mind he would have understood.'

'He was here for almost a year,' he said gently. 'We tried. He simply didn't see it, or didn't agree with it. He knew all the rules and theory. He knew how it was supposed to work, and he tried and tried to make things go according to his pre-set notions from the books. It doesn't work that way in real life. There are too many variables and they keep shifting. There are no rules that apply everywhere all the time. He wasn't flexible. I think he was afraid to deviate from what he knew and understood.'

She was silent. It came back to her in flashes—bits of memories: Matt's frustrations, his intolerance of what he called other people's interference, their ignorance.

'All of this, Rae, has nothing to do with whether he was a good man or a good husband. I am not trying to make him seem like an inferior human being, because he wasn't. He was just doing the wrong thing in the wrong place. He didn't belong here. He belonged at the university.'

'He didn't want to be at the university,' she said dully. 'He wanted to be here. He wanted to work in the Far East. He grew up. . .his father. . .' she faltered, feeling a helpless defeat. She shrugged and looked at him bleakly. 'It doesn't matter any more, does it? Matt is dead and I should just leave the past to the past.'

'The past is part of us.'

She looked at him, thinking of his wife.

'But we can't change it.'

'No, but we can come to terms with it.'

She closed her eyes. 'Yes, I'll have to try.' She came to her feet slowly. Suddenly she felt old and weary and full of sadness and regret. 'I'll go now.'

He stood there looking at her with an unfathomable expression in his eyes, saying nothing.

Come to terms with the past, Jason had said. She could no longer fail to see the truth, no longer fail to accept it. Matt had been put in the wrong place and he'd been too blind to see it. His failure had devastated him and it had been unnecessary, ending in a tragedy that should never have been.

And all the misery of the past months had been
unnecessary as well. Going over all that had happened
between herself and Jason, there was another truth
Rae needed to face: she had accused him falsely. She
had accused him, by inference, of being responsible for
Matt's death.

She couldn't sleep, and she sat on the veranda in the
warm night air, the thoughts whirling around in her
head with maddening speed. How could she have ever
done something so incredibly awful? Nobody had been
responsible for Matt's death but Matt himself.

Jason had done what he had had to do. Why had he
never told her the facts? Why had he let her think for
all those months that she was right in her assumptions?
Why?

The mosquito coil next to her chair sent up its lazy
swirls of smoke and the scent of it was in her nose.
Insects buzzed and chirped in the night and no noises
came from the kampong below. It was a clear night full
of white stars and a limitless sky that seemed to beckon
her.

For a long time she sat huddled in her chair, staring
at the stars, her body exhausted, her mind awake with
too many memories, too many regrets.

Before the dawn streaked the sky with the first light,
the muezzins began their chanting from the minarets,
an odd monotonous wail in Arabic that she could not
understand. In the kampong people began to stir.

Soon, pale light washed the sky a pearly grey, and
Rae, unmoving in her chair, watched the world come
to life. The sound of roosters crowing, the first birds.
People were coming out of their small houses to wash
in the courtyards before going to the temples for
prayers.

Why had Jason not told her about Matt? The night
had not given her the answer, and the question loomed
ever larger in her mind. It made no sense. He had

wanted her all those months, yet the facts that could have made him blameless he had kept to himself. He had never said anything against Matt, never given her any indication of the real reason for buying him out of his contract.

And it had kept her from loving him. She had wanted to, oh, she had wanted to! But there had been too much in the way, a massive mountain she couldn't go around or over.

She hugged her knees and moaned. She would have to go to him and apologise, somehow, for all the terrible things she had said to him, for all the unde-served anger she had directed at him. She wanted to know why he hadn't told her.

It wouldn't be easy to gather the courage to go to him another time, to face him and ask his forgiveness. She had once vowed she would never forgive him for what he had done to Matt. How could he ever forgive her now? She hugged her knees tighter into her chest, her stomach churning with anxiety.

Tomorrow, she said to herself. Tomorrow I'll go to him.

The sun slipped out over the horizon, bathing the world in a golden glow, bringing out the colours, as if touching them with a magic wand.

Of course, tomorrow was already here.

It was Monday and she had to wait until the afternoon when he would come back from work. She didn't know how she managed to get through the morning and teach. She was on automatic pilot, because her mind was not in the classroom with her students. She was exhausted from lack of sleep, and the heat and humid-ity drained her. After lunch she fell into bed and slept for two hours, then awoke, feeling like death. She went to the phone and dialled Jason's number. She wanted to know first if he was willing to see her, and over the phone it would be easier.

Her heart contracted at the sound of his voice, deep and familiar.

'Jason, it's Rae.'

There was a silence. 'Yes.' he said at last.

'I'd like to ask you out to dinner,' she said, in a flash of inspiration.

'Dinner?'

'As in food, restaurant. Like the *warung* on Jalan Gadjamata.' The place he had taken her to when he had apologised to her. Surely he remembered that? Only she supposed her sins were a lot worse than his. 'Jason,' she went on desperately, 'I want to apologise.' She bit her lip, gathering courage. 'I would like to see you. Talk to you.' She closed her eyes, praying he wouldn't say that they'd talked enough and he had no interest in seeing her now or ever.

'All right.' He sounded tired. 'But we'll have to skip the restaurant. I can't leave; there's no one here tonight to stay with Anouk.'

'I don't care about eating out, Jason. I was just saying it to. . .to. . .'

'I know.'

She wondered if she heard a smile in his voice. 'Can I come now?' she asked. The sooner it was over, the better.

'How about tonight? Miranda is here to play with Anouk now, and it's probably better to wait till dinner's over and Anouk is in bed.'

'Of course. Is eight-thirty all right?'

'Fine.'

'I'll see you then.' She replaced the receiver, feeling weak with relief. She went into the kitchen and drank a glass of water, then leaned her forehead against the refrigerator door. All she had to do was wait.

The minutes crept by excruciatingly slowly, but

finally it was time to go. She walked along the dark street, going slowly, suddenly not sure she had the courage to face Jason.

On the corner a food vendor tapped a spoon against a metal dish, an ugly cling-clang that notified the people that he was there if they wanted his food. By the light of a small oil lamp, he was roasting *saté* on tiny bamboo skewers over a small charcoal burner. The meat was highly peppered and deliciously spicy. Rae had bought his food several times, and he had told her that he'd pushed his little cart up the hill from the kampong for more than three years.

'*Selamat malam*,' he said and smiled at her. He was probably in his thirties. He wore patched jeans and a faded cotton shirt, and his feet were adorned with rubber thongs. Somewhere in the kampong he had a wife and three children, or so he had told her one time.

She passed him and went around the corner to the house, saying good evening to the watchman who was sitting at the gate talking with two of his friends.

Jason opened the door. 'Come on in.' He led her to the veranda and told her to sit down.

'Can I get you something to drink?' he asked, and she shook her head. She just wanted to get this over with.

He sat down, folding up the *Herald Tribune* he'd apparently been reading, and putting it down under the table.

'I came to apologise,' she said, fighting for control. 'I've said terrible things to you, and I know I can never take those back.' She bit her lip. 'I only hope you can forgive me.'

'It was a bad set of circumstances,' he said. 'I'm not angry at you, Rae. Oh, I was, at times, but that's not what this was all about. It wasn't about anger; it was about love, and what we do when we get hurt.'

'Oh, Jason,' she said, her voice quavering, 'why

didn't you tell me about Matt? You knew the truth all the time, and you never told me. All this time I thought all these terrible things about you and you just let me think them. Why? Why didn't you tell me?'

He smiled ruefully. 'I wanted to tell you, believe me. On several occasions I nearly did. Rae, I love you, and I didn't want to hurt you. I never wanted that. You loved your husband, and you believed in him so completely that there was no way I could tell you without shattering you. I didn't want you for myself at the cost of your memories. I respected your loyalty, and. . .' he shook his head '. . .it made me love you even more, strange as that may seem. If there isn't loyalty in love, then what worth does it have?'

'Oh, Jason. . .' Tears crowded her eyes. 'I'm so sorry for all this, so terribly sorry. I don't know what to do any more.'

He came to his feet and reached for her hands. 'Let me tell you what to do.'

She stood up and looked up at him, but his face was a blur. 'What?'

His arms came around her and he held her close. 'Give us another chance. Let the past be the past. Let's start over and let the future just be for you and me.'

She pressed her cheek against his chest. 'Oh, Jason, I want to, I want to so much. I'm so tired of feeling unhappy and angry. It was so awful, not loving you.' Her voice broke. 'I wanted to, but I couldn't let myself.'

'I know,' he said gently. 'I know. But you can now.'

'Yes.' Joy flooded her and she lifted her face to his and smiled.

His eyes darkened as he held her gaze. 'Tell me,' he said huskily.

She wanted nothing more. 'I love you. I love you, Jason Grant.'

'Show me,' he said huskily.

* * *

'Did your house get broken again?' Anouk wanted to know the next morning. Her face registered a mixture of delight and worry when she found Rae at the breakfast table again.

Rae laughed. 'No. We've decided I should live in your house, after all.'

'Really?' The grey eyes grew wide with happiness. 'Oh, that is wonderful!' Then her eyes narrowed and she gave the two of them a shrewd look. 'Are you going to marry with each other?'

Jason laughed. 'How would you feel about that?'

Anouk frowned, thinking hard. 'It would be fair,' she said then.

Jason glanced at Rae, then back at his daughter. 'Fair?'

She nodded. 'I talked about it with Miranda. Mrs Smith. . .she. . .you have no husband and no children. And you, Papa, you have me, but, but. . .' She hesitated for a moment, her cheeks red with the difficulty of putting everything into words. 'You have no woman. . .wife, because that was Mama and she's dead and. . .and I have no mother.' She dropped her gaze to her plate, as if she wasn't sure she should have said what she had said. 'I think it would be fair,' she said on a low note. 'We fit together.'

Rae didn't trust herself to speak. She looked at Jason and he smiled at her, then at his daughter's bent head.

'I think we fit together perfectly,' he said. 'Only you can't keep calling her Mrs Smith. She'll be Mrs Grant, but I don't think that's what you want to call her, either.'

Anouk glanced furtively at Rae. 'You'll be my new mother,' she said on a low note.

'If you want me to be. Or you could call me Aunt Rae, if you like that better.'

'No.' She shook her head determinedly. 'I have already three aunts.' Her tone was more confident now. 'I want a mother.' She paused, taking a deep breath. 'Can I call you Mom, like the American kids do? It's not the same as Mama, but almost.' Suddenly, as if a new thought had occurred to her, she gave Jason a stricken look. 'Mama won't mind, will she?'

He shook his head. 'No, Anouk, she won't mind.'

Rae watched the two, feeling happiness swell inside her like a warm tide. They were hers now—the big man with his blue eyes and his little red-haired daughter. The three of them together made a perfect fit.

GREAT SPRING READING SELECTION

NEW AUTHOR SELECTION 1990

ADORING SLAVE
Rosemary Gibson

AFTER THE AFFAIR
Miranda Lee

CONDITIONAL SURRENDER
Wendy Prentice

STUDY IN LOVE
Sally St. John

Don't miss out on this unique presentation of four new
exciting Mills & Boon authors, carefully selected for
creating the very best romantic fiction. Packed with drama
and passion, these novels are guaranteed to keep you
turning the pages.

Published: April 1990   Price: £5.40

*Available from Boots, Martins,
John Menzies, W.H. Smith, Woolworths
and other paperback stockists.*

Mills & Boon

HELP US TO GET TO KNOW YOU

and help yourself to "Passionate Enemy" by Patricia Wilson

Patricia Wilson's classic Romance isn't available in the shops but can be yours FREE when you complete and post the simple questionnaire overleaf

— Romance Survey —

If you could spare a minute to answer a few simple questions about your romantic fiction reading, we'll send you in return a FREE copy of "Passionate Enemy" by Patricia Wilson.

The information you provide will help us to get to know you better, and give you more of what you want from your romance reading.

Don't forget to fill in your name and address – so we know where to send your FREE book!

SEE OVER

Just answer these simple questions for your FREE book

1 Who is your
favourite author? _____

2 The last romance you read
(apart from this one) was? _____

3 How many Mills & Boon Romances
have you bought in the last 6 months? _____

4 How did you first hear about Mills & Boon? *(Tick one)*
❑ Friend   ❑ Television   ❑ Magazines or newspapers
❑ Saw them in the shops   ❑ Received a mailing
❑ other *(please describe)* _____

5 Where did you get this book?

_____

6 Which age
group are you in?
❑ Under 24   ❑ 25-34   ❑ 35-44
❑ 45-54   ❑ 55-64   ❑ Over 65

7 After you read your
Mills & Boon novels,
what do you do with them?
❑ Keep them   ❑ Give them away
❑ Lend them to friends
❑ Other *(Please describe)*
_____
_____

8 What do you like about Mills & Boon Romances?

_____

9 Are you a Mills & Boon subscriber?   ❑ Yes   ❑ No

*Fill in your name and address, put this page in an envelope
and post TODAY to:* **Mills & Boon Reader Survey,
FREEPOST, P.O. Box 236, Croydon, Surrey. CR9 9EL**

**NO
STAMP
NEEDED**

Name (Mrs. / Miss. / Ms. / Mr.)_____

Address _____

_____

_____ Postcode _____

PWQ1